THE SLEEPING PARTNER

'When someone isn't home when you expect them to be, and when after a decent interval they still don't turn up and send no message and have left no note, it's natural to get anxious. But there's still a lack of decisive event. There's no exact moment before which it is silly to ring the police or the nearest hospital and after which it is silly not to. Your ears are all the time waiting for the click of the door, the quick familiar footsteps and the breathless glovepeeling apology. So I didn't do anything more to find her all night.'

'Tense suspense thriller with strong and death-wishful under-tones.'

Observer

'Has Lynn been driven away by her husband's preoccupation with his experiment, or by his friendship with the pretty laboratory assistant who has a dying husband? If so, why do the police become interested in her disappearance? Here is an absorbing mystery, and an impressive psychological study with a moving love story.'

Daily Telegraph

The Sleeping Partner

WINSTON GRAHAM

THE BODLEY HEAD
LONDON   SYDNEY
TORONTO

For Tony and Tony

1

The night Lynn left me I got home quite late, but, it being
July, there was still daylight left; and I remember as I came
up the drive thinking that since we moved here I'd had no
time at all to do any of the things I'd planned when we
bought the place, such as rooting up all the laurels and
putting in some decent flowering shrubs instead.

The garage doors were open and I tapped my horn as I
drove in. I knew I wouldn't be popular, but I ran up the steps
and pushed open the front door and walked in with my usual
whistle. I hoped at least that she hadn't waited for her own
meal. It was semi-dark in the house and no lights. She
didn't answer and I thought she hadn't heard, so I
whistled again and went into the drawing-room, the room
she'd had decorated according to her own design. There
was no one there, but at the back now I could hear Kent
barking a welcome.

I wished Lynn hadn't taken against Kent so much; he was
a bull-terrier we'd more or less inherited from my sister
when she went abroad. I went through into the kitchen
switching on the lights and found the electric oven cold and
no evidence of dinner. The picture then began to come in
quite clearly that my wife was not here.

With so much on hand I might have forgotten something,
and as I went upstairs I tried to remember whether she'd said
anything before I left. I went into our bedroom with its
eggshell-blue wallpaper and off-white hangings, through to
the spare room done rather less sumptuously and to the
second and third spare rooms, not yet done at all, and back
to our wildly extravagant bathroom with its crimson ceiling
and blueberry walls. Then I went downstairs again and let
Kent out, and he licked me madly all over. That of course
was what Lynn didn't like about him; he was a delayed

7

adolescent and at five years of age still flung himself about in ecstasies of juvenile enthusiasm.

It seemed likely she'd gone out somewhere and been delayed—perhaps she had phoned the works after I left and home before I got here. She hadn't gone by car because the little M.G. was in the garage.

The right thing now was to get my own meal and have enough ready for her if by any chance she needed something when she came in. I turned to in the kitchen, assisted by Kent who slid between my legs every time I walked across the place. In the end I fired him out and got on much better.

Because I didn't know if she'd be back I went to a lot more trouble than I might have done—not just a boiled egg on a napkin-cloth spread on a corner of the kitchen table. I even got up a bottle of wine from the cellar and did the thing in style. After supper I had a cigarette and switched on the television but it was pretty grim; then I looked at my watch and saw it was ten-thirty.

I rang up her mother. It was a doubtful shot as they didn't get on particularly well, but I had to start somewhere. Mrs. Carson said in an aggrieved voice that she hadn't seen or even had a call from Lynn for over five weeks. I tried Simon Heppelwhite next and found him at home.

He said, lisping, slightly pontifical: 'Lynn? No, Michael. Not since—well, it must be only twice since the night at Quaglino's. Is anything wrong?'

'No, of course not. I was expecting her back and wondered if she might have taken root at your studio.'

'I only wish she came more often, these days. But she seems to have matters of more importance on her mind.'

'What sort of matters?'

'I hadn't paused to consider. I imagined it was looking after you.'

Because I knew him so well I thought I noticed something in his voice and persisted. 'Seriously, Simon. I can't see your face, but if Lynn's sitting there with you now . . .'

'No, Michael; seriously, Lynn isn't here and hasn't been. I'd help you if I could.'

8

After a minute or so I hung up, feeling rather a fool. I decided not to try anyone else or I should look still more of an idiot bleating because his ewe lamb was out of his sight. I waited till eleven and then thought of our daily woman, Mrs. Lloyd, in the village. But now it was too late.

It occurred to me that Lynn really had only a few close friends. There was a girl called Hazel Boylon who had worked at the same time for Simon Heppelwhite; they had kept up with each other when they both left; but I didn't know her telephone number or even her address.

The phone went. I was across the room very quickly and took up the receiver. 'Hullo!'

'Is that Mr. Granville?' A man's voice.

'Yes?'

'Oh, Mike. This is Frank.'

'Who?'

'Frank Dawson, of course.'

From the factory. Fire, burglary, accident. 'What is it?'

'Not in bed, are you?'

'No, of course not.'

'Sorry to be a bore. I was going to leave it till the morning but——'

'What?'

'I say I was going to leave it till the morning, but I wanted a private word about Read, and in the mornings he's usually hanging around. . . . Is Lynn with you?'

'Lynn? No. Not at the moment.'

'I want to have a serious chat with you about Read sometime. It looks to me that he hasn't learned a thing from the mess-up we had in February. If he's going to go on shoving people round into different jobs all the time he'll muck up delivery dates again. You remember yesterday afternoon——'

'Look,' I said; 'I'm sorry, Frank, this'll have to wait until morning.'

There was an offended pause at the other end. '*I'm* sorry, if I've barged in on something——'

'It's not that, but——' I tried to swallow back my impatience. 'I have got something on just at the moment, and anyway it's a bit late to begin on family politics, isn't it. How about facing it over a spot of lunch to-morrow?'

'Sorry, I'm booked for lunch.' I knew he wasn't.

'Then see me as soon as I've settled in. About ten. Remind me when I get in, will you?'

I hung up sharply. If he was upset, what the hell. I thought I would make one more call. I rang Ray French.

Ray answered it himself. I could hear a piano going in the background.

'This is Mike Granville,' I said. 'I suppose you haven't seen anything of Lynn to-day, have you?'

'Wait a jiffy.' There was a pause. The piano stopped in mid-phrase. 'Shades of Carl Philip Emmanuel. What did you say?'

'I wondered if you'd seen Lynn to-day.'

'I haven't *seen* her. I rang her about six this evening but, alas, no reply. What's the matter, have you lost her?'

'Temporarily. She's probably out somewhere and forgotten the time. I thought I'd check just in case you were the culprit.'

'No, old boy. What hour is it? Yes, it's late for a little girl to be out. Sure your phone can *receive* calls?'

'Yes, I've just had one. Never mind, I expect she'll turn up any minute now. Thanks.'

'You're welcome. Oh, I say . . .' as I was about to ring off.

'Yes?'

'Lynn did say when she telephoned me on Monday something about being away this week-end. I said I might drop in on Saturday with some brand-new records she'd ordered and she said she might be away then. But of course you'll know about that.'

I said, to give myself time to think: 'Well, it's only Thursday night yet, isn't it?'

'Of course. Anyway when she does turn up ask her to ring me in the morning, will you.'

'I will. Good-bye.'
'Good-bye.'

When someone isn't home when you expect them to be, when after a decent interval they still don't turn up and send no message and have left no note, it's natural to get a bit anxious. But there's still a lack of decisive event. There's no warning blip on a radar screen. There's no exact moment before which it was silly to ring the police or the nearest hospital and after which it's silly not to. Your ears are all the time waiting for the click of the door, the quick familiar footstep and the breathless glove-peeling apology.

Especially so in Lynn's case because she always had been a thought bohemian in her habits. Once when we were engaged she'd completely forgotten to meet me, and after waiting an hour I'd gone to her flat and found her curled in front of the fire, with her skirts above her knees, making toast. She was the sort of person who in spite of being very much on the mark in most ways usually missed trains or got there to catch the one that ran on Saturdays only.

So I didn't do anything more to find her all night. I got undressed and sat in bed smoking. There was a phone extension by the bed.

I don't know what time I went to sleep but I woke up in the dark and couldn't think what was the matter. Then I remembered and sat up and switched on the light, but the other bed was still empty. It was twenty past three and I kept the light on then because by then I was wide awake and really worried.

I couldn't make out why Lynn had told Ray French she might be away this week-end; so far as I knew we'd planned nothing.

For some reason I began to think of that evening in February when Ray had first called on us here. It was the week I had had the row with Harwell over delay in completing contracts, and I remember driving up to the house in a fairly preoccupied frame of mind. As my tyres made a slithery sound on the gravel Lynn came out to meet me. She was wearing a new green frock with a close-fitting skirt that made you think of the silky sheaths of tulips.

'Darling, has Ray left his car in a silly place? It's not worth moving it now because he's going in a minute.'

She kissed me and her brown eyes went over me in the observing way they had. Ray had just got up from the piano and was picking up his cheroot from the ash-tray. He was thirty-five, well turned out, with a sleek handsome face that always looked to me a trifle unused, unlived-in—it was sophisticated, but un-modern in shape and bone structure; at odds with itself, and conscious of the paradox.

'Hello, Mike. I've come to see your mansion at last. It's very grand but I miss the liveried footmen.'

I'd said: 'All we can offer you is a liverish char and she goes home at two-thirty. Lynn, have we enough dinner for three?'

'There are a few cinders in the oven, but he says he won't stay. Self-preservation, no doubt.'

'Not won't, can't.' He ran a hand carefully over his smooth fair hair. 'I'm sorry, sorry, darling, and I'm sure your meal will be bliss. But ask me another time, please. How's the new factory?'

'Very new.' I took the drink Lynn offered me, and smiled at her.

'And hush-hush?'

'Less so than the old to look at. This is all concrete floors and metal windows and strip lighting. I rather miss the cobwebby stairs.'

'How many people have you got there now?'

'About eighty at present. There's room for a hundred and fifty if we could find them.' And employ them? I suddenly thought.

He whistled on three notes. 'Big business. And can't you find them?'

'Not yet. Letherton's a way out. Also there's a general shortage. Electricians don't grow in a day.'

'D'you go down and ravish them with your presence, Lynn?'

'I used to while it was being built, but not much now.'

I glanced at her quickly, and then spoke to Ray. 'This year it's been taking too much of my time. But I've no intention of letting it get permanently in the way of a happy married life.'

Ray looked at Lynn and laughed his infectious over-spilling laugh. 'No, I wouldn't either, if I were you.'

When he'd gone there wasn't much conversation for a bit. Then I said: 'I wish you could get more company of his sort. It's what you need here.'

Her hair looked like pale floss silk as she put the gramophone records away. 'He won't come often. It's too far out.'

I said: 'I wonder why he hasn't made the grade as a pianist. He seems first-rate to me. It must be galling to have to take a job with a music publisher when you know you're that good.'

'He was five years in the war,' she said. 'That didn't help.'

'To me he always looks less like a musician than any musician decently should.'

'That's your old-fashioned notions, Mike.'

I said: 'In one way I envy him. He's artistic, in the centre of things, able to gossip about matters that interest you. . . . By the way, it's still true what I said to-night.'

'What's true?'

'That I'm not going to let things run on as they are. But you've got to be patient for a bit longer, darling, perhaps longer than I thought a month or so ago. Don't imagine I love work all that much. I like enjoying myself. And I like enjoying myself with you. It's only a question of time.'

That evening was the nearest I got to telling her about this particular crisis with Harwell that had arisen in our affairs. I thought to save her worry, but after that I found each day's silence led to the next. Technically she was a partner in the firm with a small holding of stock from which she got enough to keep herself handsomely in spending money. It had seemed a better idea when we were married than giving her a dress allowance. Later she had seemed to lose interest and to take our prosperity for granted.

I must have dozed off unexpectedly because I woke to hear someone knocking. The light was still on but it was daylight. My watch said twenty to seven and the other bed was still empty.

I got out quickly, shuffling my feet into slippers and dragging on a dressing-gown. The knocking was from the back door and I went to the landing window which looked out over the back. I don't know why I should have expected Lynn, if she turned up at that hour, to go round to the back, but one's waking expectations aren't always in the right groove. There was an umbrella there and when the window opened the umbrella moved and it was Mrs. Lloyd.

'Good morning, Mr. Granville. Overslept a little bit?'

'No, surely, you're early.'

'It's twenty-five to eight.'

I looked at my watch and then looked at it again. It had stopped. 'Wait a minute, I'll let you in.'

I went down into the silent hall and was about to slop through into the kitchen when I saw the post had come. There were a couple of bills and a letter. The letter was from Lynn.

2

I ripped open the envelope and stared at what she had written.

'My Dear Mike,

I expect I should put this on my dressing-table or on the mantelpiece downstairs, but somehow I shy away from the hackneyed move even when I am doing the hackneyed thing. I realise that by posting this in the box at the corner instead of leaving it I may give you a slightly disturbed night—that's if you happen to notice I'm not there when you get home.

Perhaps that's the last bitchy thing I'll need to say in this letter. I hope so. But Mike, I'm leaving you. Does that surprise you? And will you really mind?

Mike, I'm the wrong sort of wife for you. You must have realised it. At least you've made it very clear. Oh, there have been times, I know, but they don't happen any more for either of us, so it's not a lot of good going on pretending. I won't be around any longer to trouble your conscience or to cramp your style.

I'm taking a flat in London for a few weeks while things straighten themselves out. I'm not leaving the address because I think you might try to see me, and I believe it would be better if we didn't meet again. If you really want to say anything in answer to this, write to the Bank and they will forward it.

I've taken a few clothes, but if I want more I'll send for them.

With regret and—still some affection.

Lynn.'

Someone was knocking. I folded the letter and put it back in its envelope. 'Michael Granville Esq.,' she had written, 'Greencroft, Hockbridge, Beds.' I shoved the envelope into the pocket of my dressing-gown and went to let Mrs. Lloyd in.

'Good morning, Mr. Granville. Nasty morning, isn't it?' She folded her umbrella and propped it by the door and insinuated herself past me. 'You never can trust those bright evenings. But the weather forecast was wrong—all wrong.'

I said: 'My—watch stopped. I forgot—to wind it.'

She glanced inquisitively at me through her thick spectacles and then at the mess I'd left in the kitchen from making the evening meal. 'I expect it's keeping these late hours. I always go to bed as soon as Telly finishes. Otherwise I shouldn't be up to see Mr. Lloyd off. I'll make you a cup of tea right away.'

15

Mrs. Lloyd was always a shade too sweet for me. I said bluntly: 'Mrs. Granville's not here.'

'No, Mr. Granville, so she told me. You'll be quite the bachelor for a few days, I suppose.'

I looked at her but her glasses had glinted away. 'You knew?'

'Mrs. Granville told me just before I left yesterday. She walked down to the corner with me to post two letters. I said I'd post them, but she said she wanted to do it herself. I expect we shall manage, shan't we?'

'Yes,' I said, wondering whom the second letter was to. 'I expect we shall manage.'

'I'll get everything for your supper so you'll just have to switch on. I'll lay it for you ready and then you can leave everything for me to clear to-morrow. I hope her mother will be better soon.'

'Yes,' I said. So Lynn had covered up. Mrs. Lloyd with her intense nose for scandal hadn't smelt this one out yet. She soon would. Presently I found I'd gone upstairs and was shaving. I cut myself on the chin, and couldn't find my own toothpaste and had to use Lynn's.

I wondered then, and tried to think it out, where the first crack had really shown, where the first wrong move was made. Had I made a bloomer in ever building a new factory with a government priority and encouragement in a satellite town, and uprooting Lynn from our tiny flat in London and expecting her to take new roots in the country? Should I have stayed where I was, cramped and rat-ridden in E.C.? But could overwork and neglect ever *really* break a marriage that hadn't got dry rot already in its foundations? Perhaps the smart boys were right and the seeds of this sort of crack up were sown twenty or thirty years ago among the frustrations and fixations of childhood.

I went to the works as usual. Sometimes when you've had a partial knock-out something goes on functioning even when the higher levels are closed.

I remember getting into the car and carefully noting that the petrol was low. And I remember as I turned in the drive I

16

thought, I wonder if those laurels will get rooted out after all. I stopped at the garage at the corner and got ten gallons and then was going to drive off without paying. The man there grinned and said: 'Shall I book it, Mr. Granville? Any time. . . . Your credit's good, you know.'

My credit was good. Different from ten years ago when I'd started with a capital of £100. It had all come so quickly, perhaps too quickly. And perhaps my credit wasn't as good as it had been twelve months ago in places where it mattered. Maybe success had to be slow to be solid and enduring; even success in marriage and in love.

It was a twenty-five-minute drive to Letherton. The firm of Granville and Company was still very much a one-man affair, and in my brighter moments I sometimes speculated how long it would go on if I took ill or was knocked down by a taxi.

There was really nobody at all able or willing to take authority even for a short time, and this had been the chief cause of the mess up in February, when the details of the move into the new factory had completely swamped me, and the production had had to be left to Read and Dawson, who for some inexplicable reason hated each other's guts and got in each other's way at every opportunity. Harwell had reacted violently—unreasonably to my view—to two late deliveries; and no doubt I'd been tactless too. Anyway it had finished our association, and the outcome had been that the factory's production was truncated and being forced into commercial channels that I wasn't interested in.

As usual this morning there was a pile of letters on my desk and I'd dictated a couple of replies when Frank Dawson came in. I'd forgotten about his telephone call last night and I didn't feel very much more patient now than I'd done then. I half expected him to pitch straight in about being cut off so sharply, but instead he said: 'I brought you this, Mike. It should rejoice your soul. Exhibit D; the fourth in two weeks.'

It was a bit of work done by a new hand and ruined by having had a $\frac{5}{16}$ screw used in place of a quarter inch. Bill

17

Read, the works manager, was trying to improve production by switching some of the workers about, and this, Frank maintained, was the outcome. I pacified him as best I could, half concerned and half no longer caring; and presently, getting precious little response from me, he dried up and stood pushing back his black hair and staring out at my car waiting patiently at the front door in the rain.

I said: 'Anything else, Frank?'

'Yes. When you've time. I've made a final selection from the IDA drawings, but I want your approval before I go ahead. There are one or two I'm not sure about.'

I sighed. Like most of my other attempts to shift decisions on to other people, this one didn't look as if it was going to be a great success. 'Where are the plans? All right, I'll come and look in a few minutes. I must do a bit of phoning first. Is Mrs. Curtis in the laboratory?'

'Yes. Do you want to see her?'

'No. . . . I'll see her when I come out to you.'

He hesitated at the door, thin-featured, bright-eyed, moody. 'There's one other thing. I've a basket of strawberries for Lynn. Home grown. They're particularly good this year.'

'Oh, thanks,' I said awkwardly. 'I—you have them with you?'

'Yes. I'll shove them in the back of your car.'

'Thank you, Frank. That's very nice of you. You must—look in and see us sometime.'

'You're a bit distant now. Twelve miles is twelve times as far as it was in the old days.'

When he'd gone I sat for a minute. I lit a cigarette. Then I put it out, angry that my fingers fumbled the job. I pressed the switch of the inter-com thing and told them to get me the manager of the Pall Mall branch of the National Provincial Bank. While I was waiting I fiddled with the piece of damaged equipment.

'The manager is on the line now, Mr. Granville.'

I said: 'Good morning. My name is Granville. My wife, Mrs. Lindsey Granville, still banks with you, I think. Until

18

early this year we lived at 5, Grosvenor Lane, off Clarges Street.'

'Oh. . . . . Yes, of course. Mrs. Granville called in to see me this week.'

'Yes, well. . . . She's staying in London at the moment in a flat lent her by a friend, and I don't happen to have the address by me. I wonder if you could tell me what it is.'

There was a pause at the other end, and then a click. 'Hello,' I said.

'Er—where are you speaking from, Mr. Granville?'

'My works in Letherton.'

'Yes, I see. Er——'

'You have her address?'

'Yes, we have it. She gave it us this week when she called in. We were to forward any correspondence.'

I said: 'Would you care to ring me back? That would establish who I am.'

'Of course. Yes. . . . Actually this puts us in rather a difficult position because Mrs. Granville left us with instructions not to give her address to anyone asking for it. Naturally——'

'I do happen to be her husband.'

'Exactly. Nevertheless in the face of these explicit instructions . . . I wonder if you would allow us to write to Mrs. Granville and get her formal permission?'

Someone tapped and half entered but I waved them angrily out.

'Can't you ring her?'

'Unfortunately she didn't leave a number.'

I thought quickly, wanting to slap down the receiver but knowing I wouldn't.

'When would you hear?'

'Let me see, to-day's Friday. Posted this morning we might get our answer to-morrow. But Monday would be safer. If you'd care to ring us again then . . . Or we'll ring you.'

'Thank you,' I said. 'Perhaps you'll ring me.'

When I put down the phone Bill Read the works manager

came in and we talked for a time on routine business; but I think I gave him even less attention than I'd given Dawson. What made me feel most sore and angry was that as early as last Monday Lynn had hinted to Ray French that she was going away; she had called to see the bank manager and arranged things with him; she had warned Mrs. Lloyd; only I had been kept in the dark. I was the enemy, the one she made plans to defeat.

I went with Read into the factory to inspect some monitors we were making for a South African diamond syndicate for fixing at the gates of the mine so that if anyone went through carrying a diamond—even if it was inside him—an alarm bell rang. While we messed about, and in spite of Lynn, things registered; chiefly that the shortage of inspectors was the biggest bottle-neck. Completed parts were piling up for lack of people with the technical knowledge to check them.

Suddenly Read said: 'What about this girl who's made a pig's ear of the delay lines?' When I stared at him he said: 'Dawson complained, didn't he?'

'My dear Read,' I said, 'Frank's been with me from the start and he has a privileged position. He's head of the laboratory and pretty smart there but he doesn't understand a thing about factory organisation. On the assumption that you do I employ you to make what arrangements you think fit. Well, make them. I can't be a universal Aunt Nellie for the whole bloody workshop.'

The saving grace of Read was that you could talk to him like that. He grinned his fox-terrier grin. 'Anyway, don't you want to know what I've done about it?'

'Not particularly.'

'Thanks. . . . In fact I've taken steps. I don't think it'll happen again.'

I went down the passage to the laboratory. Only Frank Dawson was there, and Stella Curtis. Because there was a row outside they didn't hear me come in and I stared across at her for a bit. If my marriage had smashed up for the reasons Lynn implied and not because she was just fed up

20

with me, then the job this girl was working on was as responsible as any other single thing for the break.

Or perhaps the cynics would have said it was because of Stella Curtis herself.

3

I'd engaged her in March as Frank Dawson's assistant in the laboratory. She'd come in answer to a rather hopeful advertisement I put out after his last assistant had plugged in an experimental job on the wrong voltage and blown about eighty pounds worth of valves. She was, I suppose, about twenty-six, had got a good degree and had worked for a couple of years at the Nuffield Research Laboratories at Oxford. That was four years ago and apparently she'd left there to get married. She didn't explain why she wanted a job now.

She was an attractive, pale girl with dark, curly hair, and those noticeable blue eyes which some dark girls have, in which even the whites seem slightly blue. What interested me was that she seemed to know quite a lot about the theoretical side of our work, and had even earned Frank's respect. Read said mischievously it was because Dawson had fallen for her legs; I knew it was because he recognised somebody with a more inventive brain than his own.

All the same, although I knew she was a find, I didn't have a lot to do with her personally for the first seven or eight weeks, and it wasn't until the thing with Thurston suddenly flared up that I decided that she was just the person to help me.

Thurston was a queer chap, half scientist, half civil servant, who divided his time between Harwell and St. Giles's Court. After meeting on various back-room jobs during the war, we'd kept in touch because of a common interest in airborne prospecting. With his help I'd built an entirely new and simplified type of scintillometer and had tried it out in an old Land Rover with very promising results.

After my bust-up with Harwell in February he had remained my only contact; and one day in May he'd telephoned to say was I willing to take on a rush job of making an airborne scintillometer for an urgent government requirement—if so this was my big chance, not only to see my own particular scientific baby produced with unlimited backing, but to put the firm of Granville & Co. back where everyone wanted it to be.

I didn't take long to think that over, so he came and explained exactly what was in the wind, and I had Stella Curtis in to meet him. The upshot was that when I went to Harwell I took her with me.

Harwell is forty miles from Letherton and we had to be there by ten, so she got a train from Letherton where she was living and I picked her up at Hockbridge station.

When we got there I found it was a rather more imposing conference than I'd even been to before. Dr. Bennett, who was in charge, I knew slightly and liked. Steel also was there—the geophysicist whom I'd had words with at our last meeting—but he greeted me to-day in a bluff, friendly manner as if it was all forgotten, and I was rather relieved. In addition to these two there was a Wing Commander Parkinson from Farnborough, a man called Porter from the Foreign Office, three or four minor people, and of course ourselves and Thurston.

Bennett began by explaining that certain territory situated between the Sudan and Uganda was due to be handed over to the Sudan; and although a date was not fixed by treaty for the actual transfer, it was expected to be about six months after formal Sudanese independence was granted—that was to say, six months from the coming August.

Not surprisingly, this territory had never been fully prospected—it was in any case a very large tract to cover by normal means—and recently there had been reports of uranium mineralisation. It was the opinion of the Government that we couldn't afford to let radio-active sources still technically in our hands drift without safeguard into the possession of a country which, under the influence of Egypt, might lease them irresponsibly; but before diplomacy could move it had to make sure of its facts. That could only be done quickly enough by aerial survey.

He went on: 'In the United States a lot of big and ingenious equipment has been used for prospecting ground from the air, normally mounted in a Dakota; but even if that much elaboration were desirable it isn't really practicable in the present case where we want to be as unobtrusive as possible and to use the smallest plane that will serve. As it happens, over the last year or so, Mr. Granville, with Mr. Thurston's co-operation, has been developing a new piece of equipment that he claims and we hope may be the answer.'

I didn't know I'd claimed anything yet, but Thurston said quickly: 'This is really Granville's baby; I've simply provided the basic circuits; but what we've aimed at is a much lighter and at the same time more precise instrument which is suitable for use by non-technical people and which will need little or no servicing over long periods. I've no doubt from what I've seen of it so far that when it gets through a few teething troubles it will supersede much of the bigger stuff.'

They looked at me and I said: 'The design is reasonably orthodox; its chief newness is its simplicity. And of course we're using a very much larger crystal than has ever been used before. But up to now we've only been able to test it by car. If this——'

'My department is very anxious to get quick results,' Porter said. 'It's a matter of the highest diplomatic urgency. We'd like to see the plane in operation by early September.'

Dr. Bennett said: 'What plane?' and looked at Wing Commander Parkinson.

Parkinson gave his moustache a couple of quick wipes and said: 'The stuff the U.S. use in their Dakotas weighs three or four hundredweight. The Canadians have boiled it down a bit and use an Anson. But obviously our choice of plane depends on what it has to carry.'

They looked at me again. I said: 'Our equipment in the Land Rover weighs about 100 lbs.'

'Yes, well, that's getting somewhere,' agreed Parkinson. 'The chief headache from our point of view is that none of these feather-weight planes has much of a range, and in the special circumstances of this case it obviously won't be desirable to be always popping back to base to refuel. So that means extra petrol tanks and a careful watch on every pound we carry. There are disadvantages to the helicopter, so personally I'd suggest an Auster A.O.P.9. The engine develops more soup than the earlier marks, and at the same time it's smaller and easier to handle than a Prentice.'

Steel said: 'What sort of terrain is this that has to be covered? Desert?'

'Marsh and savannah and low scrub,' said Bennett.

'Flat?'

'There are some foothills in the west.'

'Are you proposing to try to differentiate between uranium and thorium ores?'

'It's a point which has to be considered.'

The meeting went into technicalities. When it broke up I walked back with Thurston and Mrs. Curtis to another office and we went through the alterations which would be necessary in the experimental design. The pilot model would be a tremendous help, but with the modifications which would have to be incorporated I could see plenty of rocks ahead. One could almost just as well start again from scratch.

Stella Curtis had been quiet enough, but at the end she asked two acute questions, and Thurston, whom I'd always thought too rarefied to notice a pretty girl, suddenly asked her if she'd ever been to Harwell before, and when she said no, offered to show her over.

So we were taken round the 'hot' laboratories where the doors open as you walk up to them to avoid the need for touching them with contaminated gloves and the air conditioning plant changes the air forty times a minute, and then we went along to the nuclear piles, with those odd nightmare-fairytale names of Gleep and Bepo and Dimple. They're never very impressive, surrounded as they are by seven feet of reinforced concrete and looking like giant square hat-boxes that have got caught up in a mass of dials and girders, but she seemed to find them interesting.

When we left I decided to call in at my home, which was only five miles off course, and get some drawings and plans I'd been making for a thing called IDA, a directional system which had been in my lap for twelve months. If I was going to be occupied with this new thing it was time Frank Dawson had a shot at them.

Stella Curtis had been quiet even for her on the way back, and I suppose I should have noticed she was looking off colour when I showed her into the drawing-room.

Lynn always went to London on a Wednesday, and Mrs. Lloyd left about twelve, but we just caught her, and I asked her if she'd pour Mrs. Curtis a drink while I collected the 250 odd drawings that were littered about one of our spare bedrooms.

Mrs. Lloyd peered up at me through her lenses as if I was a botanical specimen and said: 'You're not staying for lunch, Mr. Granville? If you'd like me to i'll——'

'No, no, we shall be off again in a few minutes. Don't bother to wait.'

I was upstairs about ten minutes altogether, and when I came down I found Stella sitting on the settee looking at a photograph she'd taken off the piano.

For a minute I spoke to her without noticing anything and then I suddenly saw that her usual nice paleness had taken on a look like a second carbon copy. I said sharply, was she all right? and she said: 'I'm sorry, Mr. Granville, I've been feeling a bit off since we left Harwell and I——'

'*I'm* sorry. . . . Is there anything I can do?'

'I wonder if I could have a drink of water?'

'Didn't that woman give you something? Wait——' I went to the cabinet at the end of the room and poured her a brandy and soda.

She was lying back sideways against the end of the settee

25

now and I told her to put her feet up. When she didn't I put them up for her and gave her the brandy to drink. After she'd sipped for a minute or two the colour began to come back.

'Damn,' she said. 'What a fool! It's only happened once ever before—more or less the same cause, I think—disturbed night, overslept and no breakfast.'

'Stay where you are. There's no hurry.'

We were silent for a bit. While I waited I thought about thallium-activated sodium iodide crystals.

She sat up and wiped her lips. 'Sorry to be such a fool. It won't happen again.'

'Take your time. It could come to anyone. I remember when I was a kid . . .'

We were silent on the drive back to Letherton. She said: 'Were those your two children in the photograph?'

'What? Oh, no, they're my sister's. We haven't any children. Have you?'

'No.'

Something made me add: 'When you're making bits for pilotless interceptors to hunt and destroy things with atomic war-heads, the future for the human race doesn't look specially rosy.'

She looked at me. 'You mean?'

'Well, that's unless you can look on it all as a happy little academic exercise, and I never have been able to. I don't think I want to see children of mine growing up in a world of ten or twenty years ahead.'

'No,' she said, but doubtfully.

Near Letherton I said: 'Are you all right now?'

'Yes, I don't know what got into me. But as it's nearly one, d'you mind if I drop off here and I can have my lunch at home? I can be back at the usual time.'

'Where do you live?'

'At the cottage past those next trees. It'll save having lunch at the canteen, unless you want me back now. . . .'

'No. . . .' I slowed the car. 'Does your husband get home to lunch?'

26

She fumbled in the car pocket for her bag. 'Yes, he's always in.'

'Oh, he'll be glad to see you, then.'

'Yes.'

I left her there. So there was a husband at any rate. Before I'd gone a hundred yards I'd forgotten her. I knew at this stage that Thurston had 'sold' me to Harwell in a big way over this survey equipment, and I knew that the rest was up to me. I felt reasonably confident of the outcome though pretty anxious about the time element. But it wasn't the same sort of 'delivery date' as the last affair, where the factory itself had been concerned. This was a much more personal thing between me alone and Harwell in which maybe only one or two people would take any part. In spite of that it was likely to settle the future of Granville & Co.—not perhaps its existence but whether it did the sort of work I wanted it to do.

4

It was the Tuesday after that that I'd promised to take Lynn out for the evening. We'd arranged to meet Simon Heppel-white, the stage designer, whom Lynn had worked for before she married me and who had first introduced us. He was an old friend, leonine, lisping, larger than life, and still a technical bachelor although well on in his forties, so we never quite knew what he would bring along to make the table even.

To-night he came with a striking young red-head called Joy Fraser. We went to Quaglino's first. The Fraser girl looked bored at the beginning as if the company was dull for her liking; and perhaps her side of it was, because Simon always made a terrific fuss of Lynn and that left me and I was thinking of the risk of over-heating in a main power unit.

However, when Simon carried Lynn off I made an effort and asked Joy Fraser to dance. She got up and drifted towards the floor with a look more of duty than of pleasure, which must have been a pretty good reflection of my own feelings. But after a bit she brightened up and said I danced well and I said so did she, and she said how old was I and I told her and she said that made me twelve years older than she was, and I said almost old enough to be her father, and she said she wasn't looking for a father. I thought that was going to end the conversation, but after a pause she said many men were still in their prime at thirty-four. So I said I still had my own teeth, and she said as it happened she had a false front one where she'd knocked it out falling downstairs a couple of years ago.

A few courses later I had another dance with her and she said: 'Simon tells me you're practically the King-pin of Electronics. Death-rays and mechanical brains. Yip-ee.'

I said: 'It's all a question of fixing the largest possible number of wires into the smallest possible box. Glorified radio factory.'

She glanced me over. 'You don't look clever. I'd take you for a Raf officer if you were a bit sprucer.'

'I'll brush up next time.'

'Except for your eyes,' she said. '*They're* queer. They're like an explorer's, as if they're used to looking long distances.'

We went round again. She certainly could dance. I wished I could solve circuiting problems this way.

She said: 'You look to me like a man with a strong sex potential.'

'That seems to change the subject.'

'It just occurred to me.'

'Well, I don't know what your standards are.'

She was silent for a bit. 'I'm a person with a strong sex potential too. It can be very difficult at times.'

'What times?'

She smiled past me. 'I think you're very sweet—and rather naïve.'

28

'Don't be deceived by it.'

'No, it's probably part of a defence mechanism. Are you afraid of your wife?'

'If I said no you wouldn't believe me.'

'That's a very intelligent remark.'

'Does it surprise you?'

Her eyes were narrowed and slightly green in the subdued light. 'I think Lynn's a very sweet person. D'you mind my calling her Lynn?'

'I think it's only right for one who's on such close terms with her husband.'

She eased herself away from me a bit then. It certainly gave us both more living space.

I said: 'What made you fall downstairs?'

'When?'

'When you lost your teeth.'

'Tooth. Oh, I had a brown-out after a cocktail party. I hadn't learned how to handle things then. I was pretty young.'

'Yes, it's nice when one gets over one's youth.'

'Now you're laughing at me. But it's perfectly true. People grow up very quickly these days. How old is Lynn?'

'Twenty-six.'

'Well, I think she's sweet. Simon says she's very artistic. Are you?'

'Anything but, I'm afraid.'

'Perhaps you sublimate your emotions.'

'I don't think Freud ever thought of guided missiles.' At Quaglino's the music is non-stop so you devise your own exits. I'd noticed that Lynn and Simon had gone off the floor a few minutes ago, so I thought it was time we returned to base. In any event I was feeling the strain of being bright and young. But when we got to the table I was surprised to see Lynn looking angry. I wondered if she'd been quarrelling with Simon, but he looked as impressive and as unruffled as usual.

At about a quarter to one we left. While we were waiting for the girls to get their coats Simon Heppelwhite said:

'I gather your factory prospers, Michael.' He was the only person who ever gave me my full name. When I didn't reply he went on: 'It was quite a risk taking that big move so soon. Now . . . in ten years you'll be a millionaire. Like Nuffield. On the crest of a new industry.'

I said: 'You know even if that weren't a wild exaggeration, it would be quite impossible these days.'

He took out a cigarette and fitted it into his long cigarette-holder. Some people going out stared at him: he was so tall. 'Anyway, I hope that you're happy, now things have turned out so well in every way.'

It was not normal to use quite that tone. I wondered if he'd heard something about my row with Harwell.

I said: 'Isn't it a bit early for the epilogue?'

He smiled behind his lighter. 'This is still Act One.'

He was about my oldest friend and I tried to think things out before I spoke. 'I don't know how you measure up happiness; it's a pretty tall order, isn't it? I'm married to the person I care most about in the world and I'm doing the job I like best. I'm too close to know more than that. Isn't happiness a thing you have to judge at a distance? Ask me in five years' time and maybe I could answer for to-night.'

Simon took the holder from between his teeth. 'That's over-modest. And it's a depressing attitude anyhow. I think you have to claim more. Grasp it and be proud of it. . . . Why don't you take Lynn away?'

'Away? Where to?'

'A holiday abroad. You both deserve it.'

'At the moment it just isn't possible.'

He shrugged and turned back from his reflection in one of the gilt mirrors. 'It's a question of calculating the risks, isn't it? Counting your losing tricks and—— Ah, here they come.'

The girls were talking like old friends, and when they came up Lynn smiled brilliantly at me. I thought, what a hope the red-head's got, even if she wanted a hope and wasn't just being conventionally amorous.

Whichever it was, and no doubt the wine helped, by the

30

last dance at the Coconut Grove she was clinging to me as closely as a contact lens. It was three when we left them and there was still more than an hour's drive home. Lynn and I didn't talk, I remember, for the first few miles. Like a dog to its vomit, I'd gone back to the problem of how to get rid of the power dissipated in the stabilising valves in a hermetically sealed unit. Then as the traffic lights began to thin out I said: 'Simon puzzles me, Lynn. I wish you'd explain him to me.'

'What needs to be explained?'

'Well, he's such a good fellow in most ways, so full of astute common sense. Yet he has these girls. . . . What's his relationship with them anyhow?'

'Why do you think I should know? I wasn't ever one of them.'

'Good God, I didn't suppose you were. But you've worked for him, you must have seen the whole thing from the inside.'

After a minute she said: 'It suits his style, the favourite-uncle attitude, and it's good for business to be seen about with attractive women. . . . Not that he might not go beyond that now and again, especially with a fast worker like Joy Fraser.'

I said: 'Talking of favourite uncles, Simon did do rather an act with me this evening, while we were waiting for you and Joy to get your coats.'

'What did he say?' Lynn asked quickly.

'He asked me if I was happy. It's rather a mouthful to answer outside the Ladies' Cloak Room.'

'Oh, God, he can be so pompous.'

I said: 'What would you have answered if he had asked you that?'

She curled down slowly into the rug like a sleepy cat, the ash-blonde head drooping slightly towards my shoulder. At one time I would have put my arm round her as a normal part of life, but the strangeness of her moods these last few months made me hesitate. She was better again, much better; but still at times withdrawn, shut away.

She murmured: 'If I were asked now, I should say, sleepy, rather cold but getting warmer, pleasantly tired, mildly exasperated, looking forward to a cup of tea and bored with being asked silly questions.'

Before we had gone much farther she was asleep. I remember thinking to myself as I drove along, happy? Well, if I can put over this latest job . . .

But Lynn was right, people like Simon asked silly questions. There's nothing more to life than life. You can't get a quart measure out of a pint pot. Only saints or lunatics tried to do that, and I'd brought myself up not to believe in either.

What had Simon called it—the depressing attitude of the over-modest? I didn't feel over-modest; anything but. Sceptical perhaps. A very proper scientific scepticism. Maybe if that infiltrated into one's private affairs it would make one reluctant to make any big claims, even if all the signals suddenly went green.

I didn't realise then how long it would be before any of the signals would again be green for me.

Six or seven weeks later—a week only before Lynn left me—we had the fiasco at Glyndebourne. At the time it didn't seem as important as it did later.

I'd had a hectic few weeks. Very nearly everything possible had gone wrong with the scintillometer; but it was moving ahead pretty well at last and Glyndebourne was one of never-miss things in our lives, so I'd arranged to slip away immediately after lunch, pick Lynn up, change and get across London to Lewes by half-past five. In the end it didn't work that way, and in spite of cutting my lunch to a cup of coffee and a sandwich, it was well after two before I left. Then because of summer traffic I couldn't make up any time on the way. At a quarter to three I drew up in the drive and found Lynn already changed and looking absolutely beautiful in a white frock with long white lace gloves that left only about six inches of rounded arm bare at the top. Her expression wasn't right for the sunny afternoon but I kissed

32

her and told her what I thought of her looks and ran upstairs and began to drag on a dinner jacket.

At three-five we were off, and I thought we'd made up the time lost. But again I'd reckoned without the holiday traffic, and it was ten past five when we got through East Grinstead. Lynn didn't say anything, but I could see she was on wires. If you're late it means staying out until the interval.

I hogged the road to Lewes, cutting in and out among all the family 8-horse powers. It was a lovely afternoon, and the sun beat down into the car, so that I was soon sweating and wishing I could have been in slacks and an open shirt on a beach somewhere. We made Uckfield with twelve minutes to go, and as I drove into the car park at Glyndebourne the last bell was ringing. Lynn slid out and I followed her at the double. Everybody had gone in and I thought the doors were closed, but we just scraped in as the attendant was going to shut them.

What followed is no fault of Glyndebourne. Last year I'd been there to a performance of *The Magic Flute,* and it had been like hearing it in a fourth musical dimension.

But to-night I arrived in a lather like an over-driven horse, to sit in a crowded and silent auditorium so that I could hardly dare to stir a foot or wipe the sweat off my face, and had to listen to one of Gluck's most funereal operas sung in French. It was all right for ten or fifteen minutes while the thing got going, but after that it became static for a very long time; and as I relaxed in my seat I began to feel sleepy. The first two or three times my eyes pricked and closed I didn't take much notice. It would soon pass. But instead the figures on the stage grew bleary and I felt my head begin to move.

I stopped it with a jerk of the muscles. A group of courtiers had come on the stage to join the Queen and were singing to Apollo. One of them reminded me of Thurston, my Harwell friend. And one of the women had a hair-style like Anne Allen, my secretary. I spent a happy couple of minutes working out who the other people on the stage were, and then the thing got out of hand. It looked to me as if

Frank Dawson and Bill Read were there dressed up like ancient Greeks and singing out of tune.

I got a nudge on my arm and that jerked me back to reality. I glanced at Lynn and met her angry eyes. I made a little apologetic face and turned guiltily to the stage. The Queen was still there, and looking so upset I thought she'd caught me nodding too. Just in time the curtain came down and I breathed again properly and woke up, released from the dreadful hypnotism of the lights.

Lynn said: 'For *heaven's* sake, Mike!'

'*Terribly* sorry.' I touched her hand. 'It was being so hot. I'll be all right after a breather.' I moved to get up.

'You *can't* go now!' she whispered, furious. 'It's only Scene One.'

'All right. I'll stick it out.'

She took her hand away. 'Stick it out! You might be having a tooth drilled without an anæsthetic.'

'*With* an anæsthetic, that's the point. The break came just in time.'

The lights were lowered again. It was the Temple of Apollo this time but nothing apparently had moved on. I hadn't often seen Lynn so furious. Of course she couldn't be expected to understand the wear and tear that had been going on these last weeks.

Suddenly the stage blurred again. The Queen might be overwhelmed with grief but I was overwhelmed with something else. I could see three of everything, then one, then no outlines at all but just colours like somebody with acute astigmatism. I started nervously as Lynn kicked my foot, and the heavy programme slipped off my knee. One or two people along the row turned and stared. I was going to bend to pick up the programme but Lynn put a sharp hand to stop me. I sat back and stared again at that mesmeric stage. I tried to stretch my legs, which are long, and then I began to yawn. I knew I couldn't put my hand up without distracting Lynn's attention from the stage, and my jaw muscle quivered and shook with trying to suppress one yawn after another.

The curtain came down again at last. With a terrific sense of relief I was able to move and pick up the programme and I followed Lynn out. We began dinner in one of the Wallops. I was constantly disarmed by the look of her; her shiny, unruffled, almost flaxen head of which a hair never seemed out of place, her straight, graceful back and fine-skinned shoulders.

Suddenly she said: 'I wonder if we shall ever make a go of it, Mike?'

'A go? Of what?'

'Our marriage.'

I said, startled: 'We've been getting along for three years.'

'Have we?'

I swallowed. 'It was my impression. I'm sorry if it isn't yours.'

She glanced across the room; her eyes stayed there too long. Her face looked very white.

After a minute, when she didn't say anything more, I said: 'This evening I've behaved like a moron. I know that and I'm terribly sorry about it. But I happened to be short of sleep, and the rush we had, and getting so hot——'

'Oh, don't go on, please,' she said. 'Don't go on.'

As she turned, her expression was hurt and angry and in a queer way rather frightened. The wine waiter brought the hock I'd ordered and I tasted it and nodded. I'd have nodded at anything short of vinegar.

I said: 'Aren't you feeling well?'

'I was feeling well until I had to wait an hour in evening dress for you to come home when you'd promised to be back after lunch, and then had to cling to the car while you drove like a madman through the traffic, and then, having practically *run* into the theatre, being unable to keep my thoughts on the stage for a moment for fear you'd *fall* out of your seat. It *can't* go on like this, Mike, really it can't.'

I began to feel rather sick. 'What do you suggest?'

She put her knife and fork down. 'I can't eat this.'

'Try. And drink something, for Pete's sake! It may make things look more tolerable.'

35

She said: 'I've been trying for quite a long time.'

I swallowed a half-glass of wine myself to try to stop the pulses that were beating in me.

'Go on.'

'There's nothing more to say.'

'Lynn . . .'

'Please let's *drop* it now. I feel so ill I can't talk any more.'

'Do you want to go home?'

'You may as well finish your dinner.'

'I don't think my appetite's much better than yours.'

'Is everything to your liking, sir?' The waiter had come up behind me, staring at our plates.

After a while we both began to peck at the food and finished the meal somehow. When the bill came I could see a slackening of tension. She said: 'On second thoughts I'll stick it out.'

'Do you mean the opera or our marriage?'

She didn't smile. Her face didn't seem to have much expression in the wan light. Others were moving as we got up to go, and I said suddenly: 'There's Ray French.'

'Is it? . . . Well, *don't* bring him over here now'

'We can't get out of it. He's seen us.'

There seemed to be a bit of hesitation all round, but as we were all moving towards the same door there was really no escape. Ray had a girl with him of about twenty-one, with shy, short-sighted, smoky-grey eyes, and a thick creamy sort of skin. She looked as if her clothes came from the Faubourg St. Honoré but that she hadn't quite the knack of making the best of them.

'My dear Lynn. And Mike. How's he behaving, darling? Not fidgeting too much? I don't think you know Miss du Caine? Two infinitely dear friends of mine, Margot.'

He was in very good spirits. There was a sort of ease and sureness about him to-night as if he was in his true element, the music and the formality and the gracious set-up being just right for that touch of the eighteenth century deep in his sophistication. Lynn put the best face on it, but I saw him once looking at her curiously. I tried to make conversation

36

with Miss du Caine, and somehow it came out that she knew Joy Fraser. After a while we got away, and presently went back to hear the opera out.

I kept myself busy all that first day Lynn left me, but I don't think I got through much work. When I arrived home, which was fairly late, I was surprised to find Mrs. Lloyd still there. She said: 'Well, I didn't rightly know, Mr. Granville, with you going off this morning so sudden. I've been home, but I came back just to get a few things going for your dinner. And then there was Kent. I thought I ought to bring something up from the village.'

I fended off Kent's hysterical greeting. Perhaps I had underestimated Mrs. Lloyd in supposing that she hadn't already smelt a scandal. I said: 'If it were not for Kent I'd go away this week-end. There isn't really much point in staying here and it would save your looking after me.'

'Well, you know I always *like* doing that, Mr. Granville. But if you've the mind to go away, perhaps Mr. Lloyd and I could take Kent, like we did that week-end you went to Paris.'

'I should be very grateful indeed.'

When she'd gone I wandered through the house followed by Kent, shamelessly trespassing where he'd never been allowed before. Working at Letherton hadn't been so bad; but here I felt absolutely lost and desolate. Why hadn't she been prepared to face me out? Might she not at least have told me where she was going to stay? Leaving her address at the bank was exactly in line with her posting the letter to say she was going, instead of leaving it in the house. It was all like a dose carefully made up for me; anxiety first, broken sleep; then the letter, the shock; then a week-end to cool off, to lose my anger and to become amenable. Monday or Tuesday she might see me.

Perhaps on certain conditions she'd agree to come back. My heart leapt at the thought. I was still in love with her, and she knew it. She knew that if it came to the point I'd throw up even the factory to make her happy.

37

In the night I woke again, the way I'd done the night before, but this time it was with the unpleasant feeling that somebody was downstairs.

5

I sat up sharply in bed and listened. It wasn't so much that I could hear anything now as that I felt sure my ears had heard something before I was awake. A moon in its third quarter had come up behind the trees, and some light fell through the undrawn curtains. Lynn's bed was bare and formal-looking, the counterpane mottled with broken shadow. No sound from Kent, who of course slept in the outhouse. But if there had been someone about . . .

I began to sit back. No doubt my nerves had been playing tricks. Lynn had complained sometimes that we were too far from the next habitation in case of trouble, but there hadn't been any burglaries in the district while we were here.

Something moved in the room below.

I threw the bedclothes back and swung out of bed, feeling for my slippers. At the door I took my dressing-gown, then looked for something to use, caught up a coat-hanger. Pretty silly to think of, but just then it seemed better than bare hands. I got to the top of the stairs. The noise had come from the drawing-room.

I went down and half-way stopped, trying to make sense of it. There was no light, but I could see by the narrow grey rectangle that the front door was partly open. You could tell too by the fresh air coming up. I told myself that perhaps I'd not shut it properly and that the wind had blown it open. But there was no wind.

Step by step now, eyes a little more used to the dark. The bottom step creaked, and I carefully missed it. Over to the front door, I pulled it wider and looked out. No one. As I turned to go back into the house I saw the glint of a key in the Yale lock. I couldn't believe my eyes. I pulled it out, stared; it made a slight rattle. Only one person beside myself had a key.

Back in the hall I moved quietly towards the door of the drawing-room. As I got near it, away from the night air, something else came. All the time I'd known her, Lynn had used a particular perfume, made by Jacques Fath; you couldn't mistake it. I was sure then.

'Lynn!' I burst into the drawing-room.

It was darker here, the windows away from the moon. As I groped for the switch the french windows swung back. Bright light flickered on from a half-dozen small lamps. Papers on the floor.

I ran to the window. 'Lynn!'

A shadow moved across the lawn and was gone into the trees.

'Lynn!' I said again. 'Come back! I want to talk to you!' I went down the two steps, nearly losing a slipper. Wet grass flicked my ankles as I ran across it.

Much darker in the trees. The little fool, coming back in the middle of the night. 'Lynn!' I shouted. 'Wait!'

It was quite a small wood behind the house, and there were too many brambles. Perhaps I should have gone straight for the road, because when I heard a car start I was too far away. By the time I got to the hedge there was only a red tail-light, like a cigarette end, dying in the distance.

I found I was still carrying the coat-hanger, and I chucked it down in anger and disappointment. I went back to the house. Coming to it from the lawn the lighted empty room was like a stage set, proportioned, planned, but unlived-in, and for some reason at this moment faintly sinister. I felt that if I waited here I should see some play begin and that the puppets might be grotesque and evil.

Kent was barking now, the silly fool, half an hour late. What had she come back for, and why at night? She obviously intended to be in the house no time and to slip out by the front door again. Her scent was still strong in the room and I found that a small pocket phial of it had been knocked over in the desk among the papers, the bills and the circulars scattered there. I couldn't remember what she kept in the desk, except a few household accounts. Most of her stuff was upstairs.

Cold now and fed up, I shut the french windows and bolted them, threw the things back in the desk, glanced round. So far as I could see she had taken nothing, disturbed nothing. Then as I was straightening up I saw something glistening by the leg of the settee. It was one of the turquoise ear-rings I had bought for her on our first anniversary. They were her favourites, and she used them only on special occasions. I wondered in what way this was a special occasion. It was earlier than I thought, a little after two. I wondered whose car she had borrowed, perhaps Hazel Boylon's. Perhaps they had been to a night-club together and had driven out here afterwards. Or perhaps Lynn had come out with some man alone.

I spent most of Saturday afternoon and evening working with Stella Curtis and a good part of Sunday at the works alone. Because we'd been leaving later than the others almost every night, I'd got into the habit of dropping her at her house on the way home, but on the Saturday evening when I slowed down she said:

'I wonder if you'd care to come in for a few minutes to meet my husband? Have you time?'

I knew by now that he was an invalid but no more. I always tried to keep the personal side separate from work; but it was hard to say no. And anyway when I got home to-night—and early for once . . .

It wasn't a bad cottage and quite big, but the rooms were low, and as I bent to go in after her she said: 'John, this is Mr. Granville. I asked him to come in for a minute or two.'

A tall bony man got up from sitting by a fire which made the room stuffy, I thought, and shook my hand. The first thing I noticed was that he was a lot older than his wife, then that his gaunt look wouldn't have mattered if it hadn't been so papery and bloodless.

'I'm glad you've called in, Mr. Granville. I've been hoping to meet you for quite a while.'

'It's high time I did, to apologise for overworking your wife so much in the last two months.'

'I think she's enjoyed it on the whole. This week has been a little hard.'

I took the chair and the cigarette offered me, Stella stood by the window, I thought nervously, smoothing her skirt, eyes on the garden.

I said: 'I don't know if Stella has explained to you what we've been working on.'

He smiled slightly, with thin lips. 'Something of it. . . .'

'The crisis this week,' I said carefully, 'was that we got all the equipment lashed up and ready for preliminary testing, and found as soon as we switched on that the circuit was insensitive and the triggering completely unreliable. I—don't know if that means much to you, but that's the chief reason I had to leave your wife on your doorstep at well after midnight last Monday.'

'And did you trace what was wrong?'

'Eventually. The people who supplied the transformer had used the wrong core material.'

There was a short silence. Stella said: 'I thought we might have gone on an hour or so longer to-night.'

'It's time we had a break. Overwork's like standing on the head of a broom: sooner or later the handle is bound to come up and hit you. It hit me last week.'

They waited for me to explain. When I didn't, John Curtis said: 'It happened to me once.'

'Probably not with the same results.'

'With unfortunate results anyway.'

'Very unfortunate,' said Stella.

'I'm sorry. Stella told me you were not well. But I don't quite know what——'

'Oh, things will be better for me soon,' he said rather brusquely. 'It's only a question of time.'

Again there was a short silence. 'Anyway,' I said, 'perhaps you'd like to know that your wife has been absolutely splendid on this job. It was almost by chance that I asked her to do this with me instead of Dawson, my head man, and she's been three times as good as he could possibly have been.'

Curtis glanced across at Stella. 'She's three times as good at most things. Looking after me among them.'

Stella raised her head and her glance met mine for a second. She had flushed slightly but her eyes were quite clear. Then she looked at her husband in the same way.

'Very handsome of you both. You know, most of the time I only do what I'm told. But I really think this calls for a drink.'

One thing about running your own factory and being answerable to no one but yourself is that it increases your all-round sense of responsibility. When I arrived on the Monday morning the big new metal press I'd bought had just arrived, and I went along at once to the rear gates where they were preparing to slide it off the lorry. I climbed over the side of the lorry and lent a hand to see that the thing was edged down the planks successfully. Even when we got the press safely to earth there was nearly an hour's sweating and straining with crowbars before it was manœuvred across the works to the place it was going to occupy.

After it was done I walked back to my office alone. I noticed that the experimental radar job we were building was coming along fairly well. A pity in a way that it would render out of date all the equipment we'd delivered this year and all the contracts we were due to complete over the next twelve months. But that was the way it was in this business.

The buzzer was going in my office as I got in, and Miss Allen spoke through to me. 'It's that bank again. The manager wants to speak to you.'

'Oh,' I said. 'Put him through.'

'Mr. Granville? . . . This is Fellowes from the Pall Mall

branch of the National Provincial Bank. We've just had a letter from your wife, Mr. Granville. It came by the eleven o'clock post.'

'Well?'

'I'm afraid it's—not very helpful to you, sir. She simply—er—thanks us for our letter of the seventeenth and restates her request that we should not disclose her present address to anyone. I'm very sorry.'

I thought for a minute. 'Did you tell her who wanted to know?'

'Of course. I assumed you wished us to do that.'

'Yes,' I said. 'Thanks.'

'We will, of course, be glad to forward any letter. . . .'

'Thanks,' I said again.

After I'd hung up Miss Allen came in with her pad. I said: 'Not just at the moment. I'd like you to get me another number. It's—er—Purley 2108.'

While I waited I made stabs with the end of my pencil in the blotting paper. They were not angry stabs but perplexed and frustrated ones.

'You're through,' said Miss Allen.

'Mrs. Carson?'

'Speaking.'

'Oh, this is Mike. Have you heard anything from Lynn since I phoned you on Thursday?'

'Oh, Mike, I telephoned you twice yesterday but couldn't get any answer. I thought——'

'No, I was out—at the works. Have you seen Lynn?'

'I've had a letter. I had a letter on Friday.'

'What did it say?'

'Well, it made me feel quite ill. She said she was—leaving you. I'd hardly an idea in the world that everything wasn't going well between you. I was very upset indeed.'

'No more than I was.'

'Whatever has happened?'

'I think maybe she's tired of me. . . .' Lynn's mother didn't answer. 'Does she give some other reason?'

'She doesn't give her reasons at all. You might know that.

It's years since she consulted me or asked my advice about anything.'

I said: 'Does she give her address in London?'

'Yes, she does. I've written to her. I said to her I couldn't understand it at all, and I didn't think——'

'What is her address?'

'Oh, Mike, she told me not to tell you. That was the last thing in her letter. I'll be writing to you, she finished, perhaps next week——'

'Don't you think I'm entitled to know?'

'It isn't what I think, dear. I certainly think she should never have left you. . . . Mike?'

'Yes?'

'Is there another woman in it—or another man?'

'There certainly isn't another woman.'

'Thank goodness. Then it may be patched up.'

'It may be patched up. There's more likelihood of that if I can go and see her instead of being kept at arm's length by this damned silly secrecy.'

'Are you telling me the absolute truth?'

'Yes.'

'Well, it's—9a, Grosvenor Court Mews, W.1. Mike, dear, if you do go, don't tell her where you got the address. Whatever happens between you and her afterwards, if she knew she'd never speak to me again.'

'I promise.' Yet, I thought swiftly, Lynn might have known her mother wouldn't keep information like that to herself—in any minor squabble she'd always favoured me. If Lynn had not wanted me to know . . .

'If I might give you a word of advice, dear . . .'

'Well?'

'Be firm with her. I never could be firm enough.'

I said: 'Nor I.'

'Perhaps that's it. Ever since she was a girl. And I never was able to argue with her without her making me feel pompous and Victorian. It's a way she has that puts you in the wrong.'

When I'd rung off I stared at the address scribbled on the

memo pad. She'd gone to earth very much where one would expect. But now that I had the address I hesitated whether to use it. The episode of Friday night was heavy on my mind. Clearly she'd not been willing to face me then. What *earthly* good would it do forcing myself on her if she were in that mood? Perhaps I too had to pick and choose the time of meeting.

6

When I drove back to Hockbridge the afternoon's post lay ungathered on the floor and I picked it up, half hoping. But no luck. A driving licence reminder, the bill for a ton of winter anthracite we'd had in last week, a letter from someone in Southsea who described himself as a gentleman and offered to make my fortune with a pools syndicate.

I got a snack supper—corner of the kitchen table this time—drank rather a lot of whisky and went early to bed. I slept fitfully, dozing and waking, dozing and dreaming. Twice I thought I heard noises and went downstairs. But this time there was no one there.

The next day at the office I decided to write to her after all and keep the fact that I knew where she was as a last resort. But it was no use. My own feelings were so ravelled up I couldn't take any line. One time I began like a pompous ass, standing on my dignity; the next I seemed to be crawling.

That evening I may have been driving a bit faster than usual but a small boy on a fairy cycle suddenly came wobbling out of a side turning right in front of me. There was about two feet to swerve without hitting a lorry and I took twenty-three inches of it. All the same the boy lost his balance and hit me as I came to a stop and collapsed in the road on top of his bike. There was rather a fuss then because a car behind nearly butted into me. Stella Curtis and I picked the boy up from among his bike. He was only about eight and scared but we couldn't find a bruise on him. His front wheel was bent like a trick cyclist's and there was a lovely long scratch down my rear wing.

After a good bit of talk the lorry and the other car went off, and I straightened the kid's wheel and asked him where he lived, and then took him along to see his mother and advised her that if she didn't want to be bereaved she should keep a boy of that age off the main road. The queer thing was that she didn't seem much upset and just kept saying in a wet voice: 'Well, I have warned 'im. He did oughter know better but he just won't be told.'

We drove on. I said: 'My mouth tastes of pennies. Release of adrenalin or something.'

She said: 'You were lovely with the small boy. Most men would have raved.'

'Better if I had. Obviously she wasn't going to.'

When we got to her house she said: 'Do come in. You must need a drink.'

'Well, I don't know if . . .'

'John would like to see you again. He hasn't been well this week and you'd cheer him up.'

Cheer him up, I thought, that was comic. 'Is he seriously ill?'

'It's a form of anæmia.'

'Quite bad?'

'Yes, quite bad.'

So I went in again, and eventually found myself staying to supper. I wasn't particularly attracted to John Curtis. He was quite impressive but I suspected him of being very much the professional sick man; and it didn't seem a happy arrangement that a girl like Stella Curtis who was young and a looker should be tied to someone twenty years older than herself and very much of an invalid, who lived in an over-warm house and was perpetually chilly, had to have his slippers put on, his pipe fetched, his chair fixed. That was the impression I got; but the talk and the company did me good. I found when she was away from the laboratory atmosphere that Stella was quite different, eager, amusing,

46

easy to be with; also whether you liked John Curtis or not, you didn't doubt his headpiece. More than once I found myself out of depth and glad to make for the shore.

I wondered what he'd been before he cracked up. Just before I left, the talk came round to the kid we'd nearly knocked down, and Curtis said: 'Stella tells me you think it a mistake to have children these days.'

So she'd told him that, had she? 'It's a matter of opinion.'

'Because of the risk of atomic warfare?'

'That among other things.'

'But life never has been without risk, has it? Every generation has its own hazards.'

'None quite so much as this, I'd say.'

He narrowed his thin brows. 'In most centuries until this one, if you had ten children and four grew up, you were doing pretty well. Then, having grown up, blood poisoning, typhus and cholera were probably as lethal as most of the risks of to-day.'

I said: 'Perhaps I take this too personally. But you see for to-day's generation I'm concerned with lining up some of the potential cholera.'

After a minute he said: 'I don't think you take it too personally. I wonder if you take it personally enough.'

'What d'you mean?'

'Well, doesn't it rather depend on the value you set on life? If life has any value at all, then it's worth creating.'

'Even if it's burnt up in a single explosion that destroys the world?'

He took out his pipe and tapped the dead tobacco into his hand. 'Well, even supposing that does happen—and there's no certainty that it will—the importance of being alive and what we do with our existence up to that moment hasn't been lost—surely. We're part of an evolutionary process. The end of the material experiment doesn't necessarily mean the end of the spiritual one.'

'Doesn't it?'

'Well, not unless you question the existence of the spirit at all.'

'I think I doubt it as something that can be unhitched from the body.'

He stared at the flakes of half-smoked tobacco in his palm, then dropped them into the grate and reached for his pouch. Stella passed it to him with a swift rustling movement of her frock and then was quiet again, profile turned towards us, detached but listening.

He said: 'I know there are an awful lot of people like you about. I've met them and wrangled mildly with them ever since undergraduate days, but I still don't know how any of you work. I don't know why the wheels continue to go round at all.'

I said: 'Perhaps they go round all the better for not having half an eye on priority bookings in an afterlife.'

He smiled, the light glinting on his taut cheek-bones. 'Isn't that rather a Victorian outlook? I mean an Edwardian objection to the Victorian outlook. Oh, I understand the anti-religious attitude of people with some personal hate— too much of it thrust down their throats as children, etc. But even that's terribly out-of-date. What person under forty had an overdose in childhood?' He stopped, short-breathed.

I felt rubbed up the wrong way, partly because of what he'd said but chiefly because of the way he'd said it. 'It isn't a question of holding a grudge. It's an attitude of mind, that's all. Modern science accepts what can be proved, it's pretty sceptical but always open to new discoveries; it's never dogmatic and so it jibs at dogma in others; it doesn't deny that some spiritual ideas are good but it has no use for out-of-date fairy tales. . . . I think also it thinks that a man who does any good thing because he wants to improve the chances and the living conditions of his next-door neighbour is better than one who "casts his bread upon the waters" in the expectation that it's all going to give him a leg up with St. Peter later on.'

Stella said: 'Mike has a nice way of putting things.' It was the first time she'd called me by my first name.

John Curtis lit his pipe. I think his hands always trembled when he did this. 'It seems to me that the science that you

48

practise lets its view be crowded up by the non-important things. Your science sees a religious structure and works from the top, breaking down what it doesn't like until what's important is buried in the ruins. My science would ignore any religious structure that exists and would work from the bottom building up. It then might find—I think it does find—that the thing it has built, entirely on scientific premises, has an extraordinary identity with nearly all the religious structures that man has been evolving ever since he crept out of the cave.'

I wondered what he meant by scientific premises—half-baked assumptions?—but I could hardly ask. I said: 'What change would it make in me if I threw over my sceptical outlook and accepted all the myths?'

'I don't particularly want you to. But I do think it vitally important that men like you, the crowned heads of the future, shouldn't restrict yourselves to a narrow technical view of life, where you can't see the wood for the trees, or the idea for the wires, or the opportunities for the dangers.' He stopped and looked at his pipe. 'You think I'm riding some private hobby-horse of my own?'

I had to say no.

'Perhaps it's true. Certainly I think it's important. I'm not talking quite so much about the pure scientist—he usually sees the mystery behind the technical tricks—it's the applied scientist who's the danger. Either he works blindly on, preoccupied with his mechanical devices, or he is sensitive enough, as you are, to lift his head from time to time and see the material world he's creating. Then he thinks life is not so much a trust to be handed on as a sordid and nauseating mistake that can't be explained.'

I left soon after. Stella walked with me to the gate. She said: 'Sorry about that. We don't often go in off the deep end.'

'I hope I haven't tired him.'

'No, I'm sure not.'

'This life must be pretty heavy on you.'

'What, looking after him?'

'And doubling with me at full stretch too.'

49

She said: 'I haven't said thanks for the testimonial the first time you came.'

'What? Oh. . . . It's only the truth. I'd never have believed a woman could have stuck at it so well.'

'I don't think I like that as much.'

'And now, seeing your home life . . .'

'What's wrong with my home life?'

'From one point of view, nothing at all. But you can't pretend it's particularly restful.'

We had got to the gate. She said rather formally: 'I hope your wife won't be annoyed at our keeping you so long.'

'She won't because she isn't there to get annoyed.'

'Oh, I see. Well . . . good night.'

'As a matter of fact, she's left me.' I don't know why I said it then; but it came out.

Stella said lightly: 'How long is she going to be away?'

'So far as I know at the moment she isn't coming back.'

There was a longish silence. When she didn't speak I said: 'One sometimes *blurts* out these embarrassing confidences.'

'. . . Are you serious?'

'Oh, quite serious, yes.'

'I *am* sorry.'

'Thanks.'

'When was it?'

'Thursday last.'

'Did you—know it was coming?'

'No. I've been more than usually dull. Maybe it's this preoccupation with technicalities your husband spoke of.'

'So sorry about that. . . . But naturally we never guessed . . .'

'Well you couldn't be expected to.' I opened the gate. 'Keep this to yourself, won't you? I'm not looking for shoulders to weep on.'

'I can only say again, I'm sorry.'

'That's all there is to say.'

In the middle of the night I thought, what a fool I am standing on my dignity, she'd be right to think me pompous

50

and stuffy. Besides, how do I *know* what she's feeling? On Friday night she'd have thought it humiliating to be caught. But perhaps really she's wanting to make this thing up and only won't make the first move.

I got up and put on a dressing-gown and fetched some notepaper and switched on the electric fire.

'My dear Lynn,

Your letter floored me when it came. Believe it or not, and in spite of our few recent squabbles, I hadn't an idea that you felt as badly about my neglect as you do. I suppose I've been like a short-sighted bus driver blundering on in spite of the warning signals; now I'm complaining that the bus has gone over the edge.

Well, it has gone over the edge for me. I haven't written before because I hoped to be able to come and see you and see what could be salvaged from the wreck. Don't you think we should meet? There won't be a scene. I think we've always been civilised about these things and I've certainly no ambition to change.

Darling, I know all this year you've only had 25% of a husband. If that's why you left me then I'm willing to throw up *whatever you say* and have a shot at beginning again on entirely different lines. But if you've left me for another man then it's going to be rather tough. But I still want to see you and hear about it in so many words. It can't be any worse than not knowing for sure. I'm not going to try to see you until you give the signal. You're right about that; it's got to be at your time and when you feel ready.

You left your key on Friday night, but I've put it under the geranium pot in the porch. You know when I'm away, so you can come back any time you like and fetch the things you want. You also dropped one of your turquoise ear-rings, which I'm sending with this.

With regret—as you say—but with very much affection.

Mike.'

51

7

Next morning Thurston rang to know when the survey equipment would be ready.

I said: 'The thing's still rather in the fourth-day-of-Creation stage. Anything fresh?'

'Could you get it ready for first experiments by Friday week?'

When quiet had been restored Thurston said apologetically: 'Farnborough suggested bringing the Auster over to you on that open ground you've got; but nobody much cares for the idea. So the plane's been flown down to the rocket site at Llanveryan, and we feel that if the thing could be fitted up there it would be much more convenient for first trials.'

I said: 'That part's all right.'

'I know. Actually it's the Ministry and not Harwell that's turning on the steam this time. The whole affair has become suddenly much more vital and more urgent because of this unrest there is in the Sudan on the self-determination issue. Nobody seems to know quite what is going to happen to our area. Porter began talking of its "importance to England" when he was on the telephone just now.'

I said: 'Well, I can understand that. But what do they expect me to do, lash the stuff together with string?'

'Do you need any extra help—will it speed things up at all?'

I thought round this. 'Honestly, David, you can swop drivers if there's any lack of confidence in the man at the wheel, but you can't go any faster for having two at the same time. . . .'

'No, I know that. I'm only anxious that you should put this over in a big way. If you do you'll be a favourite child so far as Harwell is concerned.'

When he'd rung off I went into the lab and told Stella what Thurston had said. She pursed her lips in a soundless whistle.

'I'll say good-bye to my bed for the next ten days.'

'No,' I said. 'Your part's finished. If there's any panic overtime I'll do it alone—or with Dawson.'

'Do you mean you're taking me off the job?'

'Heavens, no! I want you to keep hard at it till the whistle blows. And that won't be on Friday week, believe me. I can picture myself spending quite a bit of August in Wales.'

'Then as to staying late . . .'

Our eyes met. 'As to staying late, that's my affair. For reasons that you know, I've no ties at present.'

'Whereas I have.'

'Whereas you have. Exacting ones, however pleasant.'

Her blue eyes flickered away. 'I don't think you ought to hold my private life against me.'

'I don't hold it against you, but you're too valuable to be worked to death.'

She took in a slow breath, embarrassed. 'Thank you. I'm sure that justifies a rise.'

'I'll give you one.'

'Make it guineas.' She stopped and flushed. 'Sorry. But you do see, don't you, that if I'm here as an employee—as I am—you can't begin to take in all sorts of private pros and cons before you ask me to stay late or do extra work. Besides . . . I want to do it. I want to see it through.'

I said: 'It means we've simply got to throw the thing together. We must have a few days for testing here before it goes out.'

'They know that as well as you,' she said. 'I shouldn't worry.'

'No,' I said. 'I've given up worrying about that.'

I decided to spend this last rush period at the Old Bull at Letherton. Kent, still staying with the Lloyds, seemed fairly quiet, and, although Mrs. Lloyd peered at me through her microscopes when I said I hadn't yet heard when Mrs.

53

Granville was coming back, she didn't ask any questions. I thought of telling her of Lynn's key under the geramium so that she could go in and clean up once in a while, but I thought Lynn might come for it sometime and prefer no one to know. The house wouldn't go to pot in a week or so, and I could run over myself every day for the post.

Before I left Greencroft I packed a few things. I had to open her wardrobe, which I'd not done since she left. The white evening frock she'd worn at Glyndebourne twisted slightly on its hanger and that perfume came from it. It gave me a nasty turn, a sort of nostalgia, and above all a need to see her and talk to her again. I felt as if I'd thrown away all the things that mattered in life for the sake of a certain amount of not very important prestige.

On the Sunday, finding my own company suddenly just not to be lived with any longer, I rang Simon Heppelwhite and said could we meet for a drink somewhere. He said he was just leaving for the Criterion where his stage sets for *Volpone* were going up; but if I liked to meet him there he'd be delighted to see me.

When I got in, Simon was sitting in the stalls dwarfing the producer beside him like a lion beside a badger, while spot-lights were being switched on and off a bit of Venetian Gothic. One or two people whom I took to be actors were drifting about in the half-lit auditorium. I shouldn't altogether have been surprised to find Joy Fraser with him, but she wasn't there. Or even Lynn. . . .

At first I was sorry I'd come, as he seemed too explosive and temperamental to have much attention for outside things, but after a while the producer went off to argue with somebody at the back of the stage. We talked for a minute or two, and then I told Simon about Lynn.

He didn't give much, but sat sideways with his elbows on the back of the seat in front, rubbing his chin on his thumb.

'I'm sorry, Michael. Very sorry indeed.'

'Did you know about it?'

'Not altogether. But I suspected something. I think you've been wise in not following her.'

54

'Why particularly?'

'Well, in my opinion she's behaving like an immoderate little fool. If there *is* a hope of patching this up—and I don't in the least propose to guess what your feelings are for each other now—if there is a hope it lies in leaving her on her own to work this over for herself and find her own way out of it.'

I was a bit surprised at the strong way he'd put it. 'Have you seen her?'

'No.' After a second he added, lisping: 'Of course I should be the last person to discourage you from meeting her half-way. But to go after her now, to meet her on her own terms, so to speak, giving her the impression that she's more sinned against than sinning, would put an end to any hope there ever was of your coming satisfactorily together again. I know Lynn.'

'Perhaps she is more sinned against than sinning.'

'Oh, nonsense.' He pulled at his big knitted tie until it came still looser. 'What woman hasn't been neglected sometime in her life because the man is buried in his work? You've *slept* at home most nights, haven't you? And has it escaped everyone's notice that you've been working for *her*? Where did she get that handsome piece of cat she usually wears on her back—or her car, or the money to decorate her new home according to her most extravagant fancy. And isn't she a partner in the firm? Didn't you tell me that?'

'She's got a small stake, yes.'

He didn't speak for a while but frowned penetratingly at the stage. 'The difficulty with a doll's-size theatre like this is one has to be so careful not to *dwarf* the actors and the audience. One has to suggest magnificence in minuscule. Tell me, Michael, what your own feeling about Lynn is at this moment?'

I said: 'I think Lynn's a person with a very keen artistic and creative side to her. If you starve that, she starves. She'd probably have been much happier with a different sort of man.'

'Such as?'

55

I looked at him. 'Well, such as yourself, for instance.'

He stood up suddenly and shouted: 'No, no, take it off! Take it off!' Some men moved across the stage and he slumped back in his seat. 'The idea did cross my mind when I first met her. But it wouldn't have worked. Any other suggestions?'

'Well, Ray French perhaps.'

'An artist, I agree, and a good one. But very much a man on the make. Anyway, she couldn't have him; he's engaged.'

'I hadn't heard.'

'It was in *The Times* recently. Someone called du Caine.'

'Oh, yes, e met her with him at Glyndebourne. Anyway, I'm not saying you or him, but someone in that general group.'

He said: 'Hearing you talk, Michael, it seems to me that Lynn has given you a very serious sense of inferiority about yourself and everything you do. You always liked music when I first knew you. Now you start apologising because you don't understand Hindemith. . . . What is this you're working on at present, this scintillation something or other? Is it on the secret list?'

I pushed down the seat beside me and rested a hand on it. 'You know uranium—deposits of uranium in the earth—give off gamma rays that can be picked up by a man walking over them with a Geiger counter?'

'Yes. I had a vague idea of that.'

'Well, a low-flying plane can take the place of a man and do the job a hundred times quicker. But in a plane a Geiger counter's no use because of the swamping effects of cosmic radiation. So this later thing is used instead.' I let the seat go and it sprang up again. 'The way you make a scintillation probe unit is to get a crystal of a special kind and mount it in a sealed box with a window at the end and a photomultiplier tube shoved against the window. The gamma rays pass through this particular type of crystal and cause tiny scintillations of light which the photo cathode converts into electrical impulses and amplifies several hundred million times until at the anode end they can be counted and

56

checked. In the equipment we're making now there are various complications, but that's the general principle of the thing.'

Simon said: 'I wonder if Lynn realises that you're a much rarer bird than she is or her dilettante friends. I know you keep it all well out of sight behind an unexceptionable frontispiece, but in fact you're a morbid, introspective, sensitive brute, with just as many peculiarities as any artist and just as emotionally involved in your work. It's a gift you've got to use, and in your ordinary life allowances have to be made for it.'

I said: 'I wonder what Lynn's doing with herself now. I wonder who she's with.'

We got the thing working by the Wednesday morning. Frank Dawson was very helpful at this stage, and on the Thursday I phoned Thurston to say that we could at least try it out on the day. I asked Frank to go, expecting that Stella wouldn't be able to make it; but at the last minute she said she'd found someone to look after her husband for a couple of nights; so in the end I took them both.

I didn't get a reply from Lynn. Every morning or evening I went over to Hockridge, but there was nothing there. On Wednesday Ray rang me at the office.

'Oh, hullo, Mike, is Lynn back at Greencroft now or still madly sowing her wild oats in London?'

'Still in London.'

'Ah, I thought so. I tried your phone three or four times. What's her number in Town?'

'. . . She hasn't got one.'

'But she must have, dear boy, she rang me on Friday. Unless it was from a call box. She's still staying with Hazel—what's it—Hazel Boylon, then?'

I hesitated. 'At . . .'

'At Swiss Cottage.'

'That's the latest information. Oh, I believe we should congratulate you, Ray.'

'Thanks. I feel quite blissful. You met Margot?'

'Yes. When are you getting married?'

'Early next month. Mike, it's going to be a very quiet wedding—Margot's as shy as a deer—but I hope very much you and Lynn will be able to come.'

When I rang off I thought, so she's moved on. I wonder why she's moved on. But in a way it was more satisfactory to know she was with Hazel Boylon.

It was the last time I thought about Lynn for several days.

8

We left just after eight. Stella and Frank Dawson shared the back seat together, and the front passenger's seat and the boot were occupied by three not particularly bulky packages wrapped in blankets which represented most of the primary headaches of the last few weeks. We were in Brecon soon after twelve-thirty and reached Llanveryan about an hour later in time for a rather delayed lunch.

Llanveryan had been an aerodrome—a glorified landing strip—in the first place; then it had been where some of the early work on guided missiles had been tried out. It was on the sea side of the Cambrian Mountains and in the winter would be a bleak spot, but Friday was such an unexpectedly hot day that one could almost picture oneself out in the Sudan.

Thurston and Steel were there to meet us, and another man, Rhodes, who was to be the pilot.

It took the rest of the day fitting the thing up, and dusk was not far away by the time it was ready. We didn't fly with it that night but tried it out on the ground. As soon as it was switched on, the rate-meter started putting up spurious counts of its own; but after a few minutes we found that one of the luminous dials on the plane hadn't been scraped clear. When this was fixed the whole thing behaved in a very gentlemanly fashion.

Stella went to bed at eleven but I stayed up talking with Thurston until after one. I had thought he intended going abroad with the survey unit; but he said he could not, so it looked as if it was going to have to stand up to our claim to be operable by non-technical personnel.

On Saturday Rhodes and Thurston took the plane up, and then I went up with Rhodes. The detector response was very good indeed, but after a while I noticed that the power input had dropped very sharply, and I switched off and told him to fly back.

It took us a time to find out that the fault lay in the arrangement to draw power at six volts through a carbon pile regulator off a section of the aircraft's battery. It just wasn't going to work, and it meant our introducing a small additional six-volt accumulator, float-charging from the main supply.

We were being put up at the hostel which was part of the old aerodrome, and it was all fairly stark and war-time-emergency style. There were eight of us altogether, and Stella was the only woman. Somehow it wasn't until you got her away from her own surroundings that you realised how attractive she was. Her dress was plain and innocent enough, but she drew the eye. Even Thurston—but, then, I remembered Thurston before. One could never tell with scientists.

Sunday morning there was fog but it cleared soon after nine, and at eleven Rhodes and Thurston took off. They were going to fly a grid pattern for two hours over picked ground. Several 88mc. radium sources had been placed in various degrees of availability, but neither Rhodes nor Thurston knew where the plants had been made.

After the little plane had droned out of sight the rest of us walked back towards the hostel.

I said: 'If this first full test makes sense I shall go home to-night.'

Stella didn't say anything but Frank Dawson screwed up his sardonic face. 'That'll cause a riot.'

'No, I've been talking with Thurston. We can be in

telephone contact, and it's only five hours to get here again.'

Frank said: 'Anyway we can't let the factory go to pot even for this job. And it soon would with Read in charge.'

Stella transferred her eyes to me. There was a look of companionable understanding in their depths.

I said: 'Well, he's only had a day and a half of working time to ruin the place.'

Frank had a sense of humour over most things, but not over Read. He said: 'Well, hell, he's like a little Czar; you ought to be there, then you could talk'; and went off hunching his shoulders.

I said: 'Frank Dawson's being very difficult these days. He might owe me a personal grudge.'

'Has he been with you a long time?' Stella asked.

'Well, yes. In fact he could have been my partner if he'd been willing to carry some of the weight.'

'I don't think he would have done as a partner for you.'

It was odd, the sense of having nothing to do for two hours. The weight lifted off your head. 'He's a very practical bloke.'

'Oh, yes, in his own work. But don't you differ altogether in your attitude towards the factory? He wants it to prosper as a factory, but it doesn't awfully matter to him what it's making—logarithmic rate-meters or brass nails.'

'Perhaps his is the more sensible attitude.'

'Yes ... but don't you see if it wasn't for you it soon *would* be making only brass nails.'

'Maybe it will even yet,' I said, thinking of the plane on its travels.

She stooped to pick a yellow daisy of some sort flowering in a crack in the tarmac. 'It's not like an ordinary factory at all. It's built round one man. Without you the place would fall to bits in a week.'

'You're being very long-sighted this morning.'

'No. But an onlooker sometimes——'

'You being the onlooker.'

She smiled, all her face rounding with it. 'Well, in this I am.'

'Have you come to any other interesting conclusions about me and the firm?'

'Not really. . . .'

'Cough them up.'

'When I know you better.'

'Don't you know me well yet?'

'Not very well.'

'You've seen a great deal more of me in the last two months than my own wife has.'

Her eyes glimmered bluely as she looked beyond me. 'D'you count knowing by the quantity of time spent? . . .'

'Not necessarily——'

'It's the *quality* of the time, isn't it? The——'

'And ours has been without quality. Yes, I see that.'

She looked a bit startled, uncertain, like someone who hasn't seen a move at chess. 'Not altogether without quality perhaps but without . . .'

'Personality?'

'Well, only in a sense. You must know what I mean.'

I suppose it was the way I'd phrased things that made the conversation important, that marked the change. Yet I couldn't say there was anything deliberate about it. The words came that way and the change took place. No doubt it was all only reflecting what had been going on unknown to me for some time, and by chance I let her know it at the same time as I realised it myself.

About twelve-thirty the fog came down again. You could feel the heat of the sun through it and occasionally see a blurred yellow disc staring. There was no radar on this disused strip, but presently we got in touch with Rhodes on the short-wave radio, and after a bit we could hear him circling around somewhere not far away. When he got down he came in swearing madly because he'd buckled one of his wheels, but Thurston was very pleased with the way the surveyor had behaved and we spent most of the afternoon checking the results.

I thought I'd leave at five-thirty but Thurston said: 'I'm

wondering if you could leave one of your people behind, in view of this new urgency and in case anything unexpected crops up. Mrs. Curtis would be ideal, that's if she's able to stay.'

'I don't think for family reasons that she'd want to stay.'

He nodded. 'Well, Dawson will do. It doesn't matter about theory: we've plenty of theorists here.'

So I left Frank behind.

The fog had nearly cleared when we left about six-fifteen. I was suddenly lighter-hearted than I'd been for weeks. The fact of getting this job satisfactorily done even against the revised delivery date made me suddenly realise how much its failure would have meant to me. I knew very well the feeling of satisfaction couldn't last against the loss of Lynn, but temporarily it was there. With an hour for a meal somewhere it seemed likely that we should be home before midnight, but after about thirty minutes' driving I blamed myself for not ringing the A.A. to see how far the fog persisted. It kept coming in patches blotting everything out, and I'd have to slow to an absolute crawl. Driving through fog in the day is worse than at night because even your lights don't help. The white line was a life saver, but after about an hour we ran on to a patch of newly tarred road and I had to stop to wipe all the windows clear.

Stella said: 'Let me get out and walk. I can guide you that way, and it may be only for half a mile.'

'No thanks, I can manage.'

We started again and crawled for another couple of miles; then it eased and we made better speed. About seven we came into a sizeable village with one or two decent hotels and I saw that it was Llanwrtyd Wells. I stopped again. She looked at me inquiringly.

I said: 'I'm going to phone ahead, d'you mind, see what it's like. It would take us all night to get home at this rate. And on second thoughts it wouldn't be a bad idea to have dinner here, would it?'

She wound the window down.

'Let's see what they say about the roads.'

62

It was a fairsized hotel and seemed busy. We were just going in when I spotted an A.A. scout at the corner and hailed him.

He said: 'No sir, it's local, coming in from the sea. They say there's nothing on the A40 at Abergavenny. But it's thick at Llandovery. I'd suggest you went via Builth and Talgarth. I've just come from there and it's not at all bad.'

'Think it will get any worse?'

'No, sir; it's the heat. It's been blazing all day in Hereford.'

I said to Stella: 'Shall we eat here? You say.'

She nodded. 'I'm hungry. But first I'll ring John and tell him we're on our way.'

'Tell him we're only just on our way.'

She was some time away and when she joined me in the bar she'd taken off her light coat, combed her hair, and she certainly didn't look like a laboratory assistant. She looked young and composed and lovely, and a stranger, as if I'd never seen her in my life before. One or two men in the room obviously thought the same.

I ordered drinks and asked how her husband was.

'About the same, thank you. But he was in bed so I didn't speak to him.'

'What exactly is the matter with him?'

'Leukæmia.'

'Oh . . . that's bad, isn't it?'

Her face was clouded and I added rather clumsily: 'We're both having trouble with our partners.'

'Has anything happened about your wife since you told me?'

'I wrote her but she hasn't so far replied.'

'I'm sorry.'

I turned the stem of my glass. 'Just at the moment I'd be glad to forget it.'

'Why now?'

'Reaction. It's getting through with this job and . . .'

'Yes, it is rather a relief.'

'Optimism has been so absent from my life recently that I'd be very happy to let it run as long as it lasts.'

'Then let it.'

'Will you have another drink?'

'I haven't finished this.'

'Well, finish it and have another.'

'No, thank you.'

'It would please me quite a bit to feel that my collaborator in building this darned scintillometer was celebrating too.'

'Oh, all right.'

After a while we went in. I ordered a bottle of claret, but after the first few mouthfuls of food I found I had no appetite. I can't remember what we talked about, but it certainly wasn't about detector responses. Once or twice I found we were arguing, as if there was antagonism between us. But it wasn't that at all. I still kept looking at her as if I was seeing her for the very first time, as if she'd that moment come in at the door. What made the food have no taste at all was the realisation that she had a good idea of what I felt and didn't seem to care.

We stayed longer than we should have done over coffee and a cointreau. Now and then a queer tense silence would come down on us, like something stretched and ready to snap. When we got out to the car the fog had gone. The A.A. scout wasn't there, but I decided to take his advice and make for Builth and Talgarth.

We'd been laughing about something as we got in but now she sat quietly beside me, her coat folded across her knees, one hand resting on the ledge of the door. Now and then she gave her head an impatient backward flick, which was partly nervous and partly because one dark curl came too low on her forehead. The mood didn't change. I tried to think of Lynn sitting in that seat as she had done so many hundreds of times, but it didn't help. I only knew at that moment about Stella Curtis.

After we'd gone a few miles we came to a signpost marked Brecon, and I hesitated, not knowing what to do, because this looked like a side road. Brecon was obviously the direct route for Abergavenny, and perhaps this was the way the A.A. scout had meant. I took the road and all was well for another mile or so but then we began to climb. We must have been pretty high to begin with, but this road went up and up until we seemed to be fairly among the mountains. It just ran on unfenced through wild open land.

I said: 'I think I've done the wrong thing. This is going over the top of the range.'

'Well, the fog seems to have cleared.'

'We shall probably end up in a farmyard.'

'It definitely said Brecon.'

The light wasn't fading yet and you could feel the warmth of the sun through the cloud, even though the sunset couldn't be far away. We'd climbed probably a thousand feet and there was rough wild land stretching up on either side. But it was as if here we were above the fog. Then we passed a couple of grim granite cottages with a man working in a garden, so I stopped and asked the way. Yes, we were right for Brecon. Yes, we were crossing the mountains. Yes, it was still eleven or twelve miles to Brecon, now. But the road from here dropped most of the time, soon we should be following the stream. Comforted, I got back into the car and drove on.

Three or four miles later, gently dropping all the time as the man had predicted, we went down into a bank of fog that you could almost feel. It was like being in a plane when you fly into a cloud, only you had no blind-approach-beacon system to guide you. A few hundred yards after that, going pretty slowly but evidently not slowly enough, I ran off the road and split my left front tyre on a stone.

9

By the time I'd come to the reluctant conclusion that, because of the angle of the car, I couldn't get the jack under,

I was dirty and hot and the light was failing. She'd done what she could to help, and now we went round to the car and sat in it a few minutes and had a cigarette.

'It's rather obvious,' I said, 'that you won't be home to-night.'

'Oh, well . . .'

'If the man we asked was right we're about half-way between Llanwrtyd Wells and Brecon. But Brecon is downhill.'

'Downhill sounds better.'

'There are really three things we can do, aren't there? Sit here and hope for a passing car. Or you can stay here while I walk to Brecon. Or you can come with me and hope for a cottage or a farm.'

'I'll come with you.'

'It must be seven or eight miles.'

'I've good shoes. And I don't much fancy staying here on my own.'

We set off. I knew she had good shoes.

After a while I said: 'I'm damned sorry about this.'

'It doesn't matter. I'm rather enjoying it.'

'Enjoying it?'

'Shouldn't I have said that?'

'I'm very glad you are.'

'It would be a pity to lose that wave of optimism so soon, wouldn't it? Merely over a fog and a burst tyre.'

'Oh, *I'm* not complaining.'

This sentence got extra meaning into it. 'Well, it's not unpleasant walking in the Welsh mountains. And it's certainly a change from Nobeloy resistors.'

'I've often wondered about you, Stella. Why you went in for this sort of thing.'

'I didn't really. It's a long story.'

'Which you prefer not to tell?'

'Oh, I'll tell you gladly sometime. But I don't think this is quite the time.'

'Or the mood?'

'Or the mood.'

'Do you like it—the work, I mean?'

She hesitated. 'Not the routine work—that bores me. I like things that have to be tackled and solved.'

'In electronics particularly or in life generally?'

She smiled. 'It reads the same either way up.'

'It isn't the sort of job one usually associates with a woman.'

'Isn't it?'

'At least, not with one like you.'

'Why not with one like me?'

'You ought to know.'

She looked at me with grave eyes. 'I don't know. I'm sorry.'

I said: 'Yes, you do know. And you're not sorry.'

'All right,' she said. 'If you think that. I'm not sorry.'

'. . . I wish we were a thousand miles from Brecon.'

She didn't speak.

I said: 'You heard what I said?'

'Yes, Mike, I heard. But it isn't any good wishing, is it?'

There was a long silence. She said: 'Perhaps it's good to wish it. Or it does me good to know of the wish. . . . We'll be among cottages soon.'

'To hell with the cottages!'

Again there was a pause. Slowly she said, pressing the words out: 'I don't think that I'm—as free as you are.'

It brought a sudden cold turn to the conversation.

'Sorry,' I said. 'That makes me feel rather unoriginal.'

'It wasn't meant to.'

I didn't speak.

'Mike, it wasn't meant to.'

'All right. But nobody will ever believe I didn't run into that stone on purpose.'

'They will if we get to Brecon.'

We walked on for about half a mile. Some sheep were clustered beside the road staring at us. Behind them was a clump of trees, in line, regimented like soldiers. I thought I heard a motor-bike in the distance but perhaps it was a plane.

67

I said: 'There's a stream down there somewhere.'

She stopped and peered over a broken stone wall. 'I can't see it. Oh, yes. It's quite close. See, there.'

'I think I'll wash some of this muck off my hands.'

I climbed through the gap and through a yard or two of stubby undergrowth. It was one of those Welsh streams that in the summer are only a few feet wide but form deeper pools here and there along their courses. I rinsed my hands, and she came and stood beside me and after a minute crouched and rinsed her own. After the warmth of the evening the water was cold and fresh. We stood up together, wiping our hands on a bit of rag I'd had in the car. We smiled at each other, companionable again.

Her eyes went past me and she said: 'Isn't that a cottage over there, among those trees?'

She was pointing across the stream. The fog had broken and there was certainly some sort of a roof showing.

'I'll go and see.'

'Wait. I'll come too.'

It meant jumping the stream, about four feet wide here, and I was going to help her but she was across before me. The shadowed blueness of her eyes showed brilliantly as she smiled at me and then began to climb the ground at the other side.

It was moorland and then a wall. This time, because it was higher, I was over first and put a hand up to help her down. She took it. Our hands were cold after the water. Then she was down and was against me. We looked at each other and I kissed her.

It was a pretty ordinary thing to happen, no doubt, and hardly unexpected after the way we'd been talking. So perhaps I was a fool for feeling the way I did. I felt as if I'd been flying too high in an unpressurised plane.

Afterwards she leaned against the wall and brushed her hair back with a slow forearm.

I said: 'That before the cottage anyhow.'

She looked at me with a sort of uplifted pallor in her face, and went on, pushing ahead of me through some thickets.

We came to a hedge and found a gap and there stopped. We'd come on a high building of some description but it certainly wasn't a cottage.

'It looks like a chapel,' she said.

'Well, there must be a village somewhere near, then.'

We went round the high blank wall. At the front you could see that her guess had been the right one. But grass sprouted between the steps, and brambles lay across the overgrown path. I went up to the door and tried the handle. It turned and I went in.

The light was almost gone now, but you could just see that the place had been stripped. And you could see the lighter patch at the other end where the roof had fallen.

'Perhaps no village after all,' I said.

'Don't go in far if the floor's rocky.'

'It seems good enough. Probably there are disused mines about. I shouldn't think this has been used for forty years.' I took out a pocket torch that I always carried in the car and shone it round.

'Probably lead,' she said. 'There are some near Plynlimon, I know. Thank goodness for a torch.'

I flickered it near enough to her to see her face; then I put out the light and moved back to the door. There I stopped. 'Stella.'

'No, Mike.'

I caught her hand.

'No, Mike.'

But her voice wasn't sure enough. I kissed her again. She felt as if she had no bones in her body.

Somehow we got out into the gathering dusk; I don't remember how.

She said: 'Let's get back to the road.'

'I wonder where this path leads.'

'Nowhere, I should think.'

'There might be a cottage near.'

We followed it for a couple of hundred yards, but her guess was right as usual. The path tapered off and ran into a shallow gully which looked as if it was man-made

69

and might at one time have had a railway line laid along it.

'Let's get back to the road,' she said again.

We veered left, in search of the stream, and soon found it. Here it was a trifle wider than where we'd crossed it first. We jumped together but she didn't quite make it and slipped with one foot. I pulled her out quickly and she grimaced and sat on the bank.

'Hurt?'

'No, only wet. And to think I won the long-jump once!' She took off one red shoe and emptied water out and wriggled her stockinged foot. I sat and looked at her foot. 'Mike, you frighten me,' she said without in the least changing her tone.

'I might say the same of you.'

'Hoh! . . .'

'But it's true. It's true.'

We stopped talking for a moment, rather suddenly, faced with an almost overwhelming sense of being on the edge of things.

I said painstakingly: 'It's queer how this has happened.'

'What has?'

'I only mean that I'm due for new tyres and they're waiting at the garage. If it hadn't been for this job I'd already have had them fitted.'

'And a new one wouldn't have split?'

'It might not have.'

'It was a very sharp stone.'

'Yes—a very sharp stone.'

I was looking at her again.

'Mike . . .'

I said: 'I'm as shaky as a man with a match in a gunpowder room.'

'Put the match out.'

'There isn't any way.'

'Except getting out of this fog.' She began to put on her shoe.

'Dry it off properly,' I said. 'Darling, darling, I'll not touch you again.'

She said in a lost voice: 'Don't suppose all the explosives are on your side.'

'I don't—I didn't—I won't.'

She tied the tongued-leather lace, her slight fingers, which I'd seen so expert, getting in each other's way. As she fumbled she lifted her head to push away her hair; her back straightened like a bow released; you pictured it quivering with the hint of strain. You could see the line of her thigh through the pleated skirt.

I got up. 'Let's go.'

We started off at right angles to the stream, expecting the road in fifty yards, but the rough empty moorland went on. Then we came to the stream again, barring our path.

I said: 'My God, if we're not careful we shall be lost!'

'I think we are now.'

I shone my light about, but the beam only reflected drifting mist.

'Is there a moon to-night?'

'Yes, you remember yesterday.'

I said: 'If we follow the stream we're surely going in the right direction.'

'But will it lead us back to the road? We've already come downstream.'

'If we follow it down a couple of hundred yards we might know.'

'Or up.'

We tossed for it and downstream won. Presently we came on the remains of a railway line. It was no more than a flattened track, with one or two sleepers deeply buried in brambles.

'We can't be far from the chapel.'

The fog had come down with the dark. I went off a few paces trying to see ahead along the old track, but suddenly she called, 'Mike!'

'Yes?'

'Where are you?'

I switched on my torch. 'Here!'

'For heaven's sake!'

71

I went quickly back and we almost blundered into each other. I took her again and kissed her face and hands.

She said in an urgent voice: 'Let's go back to the car.'

'Which way? You choose. I've persistently led you wrong.'

'This way, then.' She led the way up the railway track, holding my hand. Her fingers were cold but it was like holding a flame.

There was another building beside the old track, like a railwayman's hut, but quite a size. The door was half off its hinges but I shoved it open. This hadn't the dank unhealthy taint of the chapel; perhaps it had been used more recently by tramps. There was a fireplace in one wall and a broken lantern hung on a nail. A chair without legs and a deal table, a rusty frying-pan. A pile of sacks.

I said to her: 'Stop or go on?'

'Go on.'

We followed the track again. The stream was quite out of hearing now, but of course we could always find that again.

We went on another couple of hundred yards until we came to a broken truck on its side. Here the track branched, but neither branch looked less overgrown than the other.

'We're lost,' she said.

Being just then of that heart and body and mind, I could have said, Well done.

'What now?'

'Go back, I suppose.'

As we came to the hut I said: 'We'd better stay here for a bit until it clears.'

'How long will that be?'

'It *may* lift soon. You can never tell one minute from the next.'

It was too dark now to see her face clearly, but her eyes glimmered with what seemed to be their own light.

Her hand seemed to want to get away from mine but I held it firmly. She still hesitated on the threshold of the hut. At this point at least I would do no more.

She said in a normal voice: 'I wish this fog would lift. It's worse than ever now.'

'Perhaps we can get a fire going. There's the chair we can burn.'

'I was never good at camping out. Were you?'

'No,' I said.

She went slowly in. After a few seconds I followed her. I closed the door behind us and it nearly fell off its remaining hinge. Then I began to make love to her in there in the warmer darkness of the hut.

10

I got to the works the next day about two.

They weren't expecting me at that hour and Read came in full of curiosity to know how we'd got on. When he heard Dawson had stayed behind he said:

'I expect they couldn't resist his fatal charm. And Mrs. Curtis?'

'I brought her home. We should have been back last night but we got befogged and had to spend the night at Brecon. I suppose Thurston hasn't rung?'

'No. By the way, those two chaps I took on last month have asked me what chance there is of them becoming inspectors. I said it would have to wait till you came home.'

'Have they any qualifications?'

'Not certificates. But I thought you'd perhaps best see them yourself sometime, if you don't mind.'

When he had gone I tried to take myself in hand. I'd thought, when I got into the office, yesterday would have to take second place. But it wouldn't.

I was quite wide awake to the fact that to play up a rather phoney-looking mishap in the Welsh mountains in order to seduce one's secretary isn't everybody's idea of nice behaviour. Especially when the girl had a sick husband and was herself lit up with the wine she had drunk.

Well, there it was. Conduct for cads, Chapter Two,

paragraph one. But the corollary appeared to be that the cad felt too excited about it to be ashamed of himself. I didn't know if that was in character too. All sorts of things had changed for me since yesterday.

All right. I said to myself, you're in love. Why make a thing about it? It's not the first time. What about Lynn?

And there I struck the rocks. Because it was the first time, this way. Yes, I'd been in love with Lynn. I remembered those early feelings, even though they were as if they had happened to another man. Perhaps it was another man because they were different from these. Or was this only the second or the third of the fifty-seven varieties of love?

No, precisely no, because the physical thing of last night, important though it was, was not the whole of it, perhaps not even the half of it. I still didn't know what I felt about Lynn. She was my wife and I was tied to her by twenty ties. But they didn't affect or even touch what had come from yesterday.

For the rest of the day I tried to pick up some of the loose ends that had been dropped. In the evening I knew I ought to drive over to Hockbridge to see if there was any letter yet from Lynn, but I funked it and instead went to the pictures and spent the night at the hotel in Letherton. The next morning Stella was not at the factory.

Perhaps it wasn't altogether surprising, and yet I had expected her to keep to the routine for the time being, for form's sake. I stuck it until twelve and then decided to go round and see her. I didn't like the thought of meeting John Curtis again, but I liked still less the idea of not knowing what she intended to do.

Just as I was thinking up an excuse for going, Thurston arrived. He smiled with his tight secret lips.

'I left early this morning.'

'Why have you come this far?' I said. 'Trouble?'

'Not exactly. Though in a way, yes. Certain criticisms of the instrument have been put forward, chiefly by Steel. Does he owe you a grudge, by any chance?'

'What? I've no idea. He may.'

'What happened in February exactly?'

'Well, you know we let Steel's department down badly on two delivery dates. The firm deserved every sort of raspberry for it—and they got it. But part of the blame was Steel's for the absolutely ridiculous flow of modifications sent in to the original contracts. Of course one expects a few, but this was unreasonable. It confused my people and sent them astray. I felt pretty sore about it at the time, that the whole fault was laid on us. At our last meeting I told Steel what I thought about it. We had rather a set-to.'

Thurston plucked at his bottom lip. 'One doesn't like to think of this in terms of personalities—and of course it may not be—but it does seem to me that he's putting forward more objections in this case than are reasonably justifiable.'

'What does he complain about?'

'Chiefly the lack of a terrain clearance instrument. You know the sort of thing: a radioaltimeter that feeds its information electronically to the rate-meter so you get an automatic compensation for undulations in the ground.'

I said: 'It means extra weight and a hell of an elaboration. Just what we've tried to avoid.'

'I know. But the Whitehall boys love something that sounds ingenious and can be expressed in words of five syllables. And of course in this particular field Steel's influence is fairly powerful.'

We talked for about twenty minutes. As he got up to go I said: 'You want Dawson to stay down there at present?'

'If you can spare him. It might save you or Mrs. Curtis another journey.'

Mrs. Curtis. Mike, Mike, Mike, she'd said my name over and over again on Sunday night, in different tones and shades of meaning. Protest, affection, passion, detachment.

'I called in to see them on the way here,' Thurston said, making for the door. 'It seemed a suitable thing to do.'

'Yes,' I said, talking with him and walking with him to the dilapidated car he drove.

'I'll ring,' he said. 'Steel may have been only making

routine noises. If not we'll have to fight it out at a full conference.'

He got into his car. I said: 'Who did you say you'd been to see?'

'The Curtises. I'd only met him twice before, but one likes to pay one's respects.'

'What, to Mr. Curtis?'

'To Dr. Curtis, yes.'

'I don't quite get you.'

Thurston looked at me. 'Well, it's a pretty big loss, that, while he's still at the height of his powers.'

'I don't follow you, David. What are you talking about?'

He put in the ignition key. 'You must know who he is. Curtis of the Cavendish Laboratories. As you've worked so closely——'

I said: 'I don't know anything about him. You mean he's a scientist?'

'Was. One of our ablest. I suppose you won't remember the paper he read, two, no, three years ago to the Royal Society on "The Unity of Radiation and Matter"? It's still the definitive pronouncement.'

I said: 'Why the blazes didn't somebody *tell* me?'

Thurston shrugged. 'I naturally thought his wife would have done.'

'She didn't.'

'Not when you engaged her?'

'No.'

'There seems no reason to have made a secret of it. Perhaps——'

'Did she tell you?'

'No, but when you said you were bringing an assistant to Harwell, of course we had to have her screened, so naturally we knew.'

'Was that why you made such a fuss of her?'

He looked at me rather queerly. 'I don't know that I made "a fuss" of her. Obviously one tries to offer some courtesy to the wife of a distinguished man who has been struck down as he has.'

'*Wait*,' I said, as he reached for the starter button. 'What's the matter with him?'

Thurston stopped with his hand half-way. 'We're usually much too cunning nowadays to risk our lives monkeying about with these things without adequate protection. There aren't gamma-ray martyrs dotted about the country the way there used to be with X-rays. At least, not yet! But now and then someone slips up. John Curtis slipped up—or that's the general opinion.' He started the engine. 'I was surprised to see him still out of bed.'

I held on to the door of the car like a talkative leave-taker. But I wasn't feeling talkative. I was trying to sift the operative word out of Thurston's last sentence.

'Still?' I said. 'D'you mean *already* out of bed?'

'No, still. He's been ill six or seven months now. I understand he is not likely to last beyond the end of the year.'

After lunch I got in my car and drove to Raglan Cottage. I thought if I didn't go right away I shouldn't go at all.

When I got there a strange woman opened the door. She said: 'I'm Miss Willis. No, I'm sorry Mrs. Curtis is out. Dr. Curtis is in, but I don't think he's seeing visitors.'

'No,' I said. 'When will Mrs. Curtis——?'

'That you, Granville?' came Curtis's voice from the sitting-room. 'Come in, will you?'

There was no escape then. He was sitting in front of the usual fire, but the day was so warm that he had a window open. He was in a dressing-gown and looked like a ghost.

'Sit down,' waving the end of an unlighted pipe. 'Stella's out shopping. It was good of you to give her an extra day. I think she needs it.'

I said: 'Are you better than when I came before?'

'Oh, better than then.'

I thought, J. N. Curtis, of course. If I didn't mistake, he'd been on the War Research Council. Younger then. Younger than I was now.

'Smoke?'

'Thanks,' I said.

'Do you want to see Stella specially? She's gone to Chelmsford.'

'No. It's not important.'

'As a matter of fact we've had one visitor to-day—David Thurston, whom you know.'

'He told me he'd called. I didn't know you knew each other.'

'Very little.'

He began to light his pipe. I got up and passed him the matches. He nodded his thanks. 'I used to play a lot of tennis,' he said. 'This is the weather for it. D'you play?'

'I haven't for some years.'

'Stella's pretty good. This time last year we used to play two or three evenings a week.'

'Where was that?' I asked, groping for words.

'In Cambridge. Perhaps you'd give her a game sometime. She tells me there are courts at the other end of the town.'

'Yes,' I said. I couldn't stay here any longer.

'Before you go,' he said, seeing my movement, 'I rather wanted to say sorry for shoving my views down your throat that evening.'

'I didn't notice it,' I said, flushing. 'Anyway if there was any shoving done . . . you were at liberty to do it.'

He smiled slightly. 'One has too many hours to brood, that's the trouble.'

I said: 'I've got to tell you that Stella never told me who you were. I hadn't the *ghost* of an idea until Thurston told me this afternoon. I'm still buried under the debris.'

'It's my fault Stella doesn't tell people. The fewer who know . . .'

'But I mean merely your identity——' I stopped.

'And not my illness? Well, one goes with the other, doesn't it? I don't want to feel like Charles the Second.'

I got up to knock my ash off, and stayed up. 'These last few minutes I've tried to see myself in your place. . . .'

'It's always a useful exercise.'

'This thing you've got. What does it amount to?'

'My anæmia? An excess of white blood corpuscles. Very undramatic.'

'And what can be done about it?'

'One makes one's will. One loses one's fear of growing old.'

'Because of doing things with radio-active materials?'

He shook his head. 'I took a few chances. But that's no proof at all. It's only a theory.'

'Whose theory?'

'A medical theory.'

'Which happens to be true?'

He shrugged. 'We don't know enough about it. All we know is that we get a higher incidence of leukæmia among people who've been exposed to small over-tolerance doses of radiation. It's called a late proliferative response. The whole subject's tremendously interesting, but I certainly didn't intend to use myself as a guinea-pig.'

I walked up and down once. 'You remind me of Stella,' he said.

'What astonishes me——'

'Go on.'

'It'll lead to argument again.'

'I've still time for that.'

'What I can't understand is your being the way you are and holding the views you do.'

'I don't see the connection. Surely nobody cuts his coat as obviously as that.'

'I don't know. Perhaps nobody knows until it comes to the point. But you make me feel very small. . . .'

He had been watching me. I tried to imagine what he had looked like before he was ill.

He said: 'What I was trying to say the other night is this. D'you mind? . . .'

'No.'

'In fifteen years we shan't need coal. How old will you be then? Still under fifty? Men like you will be the new kings. That's one reason why *I'm* anxious about the future.'

79

'You don't trust us,' I said. It was a pretty queer thing to say to him.

'I don't trust you only because you yourselves have nothing to trust—or will allow yourselves nothing to trust.'

'You mean because we're atheists or agnostics?'

'I don't like the terms,' he said. 'They mean nothing. Selfishness is the only true atheism.'

'Well, then?'

He stopped. 'Sorry. When I talk too much I lose my breath. Hold hard.'

I waited.

He said: 'Science, I suppose you'd say, begins with observed facts systematically classified. Right? Well, there is one fact about man that has distinguished him from his first appearance on the earth. It marks him as different from all other creatures. That is, he's a worshipping animal. Wherever he's existed there are the remains in some form of his worship. That's not a pious conclusion; it's an observed fact. And all through prehistory and recorded history, when he's deprived himself of that he's gone to pieces. Many people nowadays are going to pieces, or they find the first convenient prop to tie their instincts on to. It's behind the extraordinary adulation of royalty. It's behind the mobbing of TV stars. If you don't give expression to an instinct, you've got to sublimate it or go out of your mind.'

'And as for us . . .'

'Well, the ordinary man has to work his own way through. I've no cure-all to suggest. What I'm concerned about is you people whose hands are going to hold so much power.'

'I'm concerned with that too.'

'I know. It's where we came in. But I thought I'd try to explain my rudeness.'

'There wasn't any rudeness. I told you.'

He hesitated, his brows together and contradicting the upturn of his thin clever mouth. 'As I see it, Mike—may I call you Mike?'

'Of course.'

'As I see it, Mike, science can't emancipate man from his own nature; it can only help him—if he has a certain amount of intellectual modesty—to understand it better. In times of crisis, if a man has no reference outside himself, even his best moral judgments straggle off into enervation and expediency. If you lose your sense of wonder you lose your sense of balance. Who was it said: "Here is a great man, here is my master—to betray him is to betray myself"? I don't think he was stating a religious fact but simply a principle of life.'

I glanced up and saw that Stella had come into the hall.

11

Meeting her again was deadly with him there. And his being there was now so much worse than I'd ever reckoned on. Somehow we got through it. She was pale but quite in hand.

We talked about general things. I told her of Thurston's visit. She said she would be in at the usual time to-morrow. John Curtis wanted me to stay on to tea but I made an excuse and left. She seemed not to want to walk with me to the gate but I took her arm in my hand.

'Stella,' I said. 'I didn't *know*.'

'Know what?'

'Who John was.'

'He likes to be close about these things.'

I struggled with thoughts. 'It doesn't, can't, change what I feel about you. But it very much shakes up the way I feel about myself.'

'I'm not very prideful either,' she said.

I stopped, fingering a bunch of a cherry tree. 'What happened, Stella, isn't pared down for me by any second thoughts I may have now. But hearing what I've heard to-day makes me feel—rather like an assassin.'

She stared across the garden rather blindly. 'You haven't killed him. Life's killed him.'

'Your feeling queer after your visit to Harwell—was that something to do with John?'

'Yes, that night he'd gone farther than ever downhill. . . . I'd never been to Harwell before. Of course he didn't work there; but seeing it suddenly like a great factory of the future and knowing what it had come to mean in the lives of just two people . . . I was nearly a casualty in the car.'

We went on to the gate.

I said: 'I must see you soon.'

'I shall come to-morrow as usual. But I shall have to leave.'

'Why?'

'We can't go on after Sunday.'

Desperately I said: 'He'll want to know why.'

'I'll tell him I'm tired, want a break. And—he'll need more attention as time goes on.'

'Isn't there anything at all to be done for him?'

'The doctors say not.'

I said: 'Stella, when things happen as they happened on Sunday, you don't add it up at the time. But obviously that . . . I want very much to know . . .'

I dried up, not able to go on.

'If I love him?' she said recklessly. 'Yes, I love him. It doesn't make Sunday any more admirable, does it?'

'Hell, I don't know. I don't know.'

She shook her head. 'There's something I feel I've got to say—even if you don't much like it, Mike.' She looked at me.

'Go on.'

'Ever since Sunday I've been thinking, trying to see it from a distance, as if it had happened to somebody else. And in a way it seems to me—how can I put it? . . . What happened happened more easily because I have been in love with John. . . . If you've been happy with love you have less defence against it. You can pretend to yourself only for so long. . . .'

There was a long silence.

82

I said: 'To-morrow?'

'To-morrow.'

'Stella, you've tried to tell me how Sunday looks to you. It isn't even necessary to tell you how it looks to me. The things I said to you then—if you remember them . . .'

'I remember them.'

'The things I said to you then I'm very much more sure of now than ever. I'd double the stakes. And double them again.'

In the sunlight her narrowed eyes had unusual lights and depths even for them. She smiled at me, not happily but with a glance of heightened sensibility that made my pulses thump. Then she turned away without saying what I hoped she might say but knew at heart she could not.

From there I went back to the works. When I got in I took out the *Who's Who*. My eyes skimmed over the entry when I found it. 'Curtis, John Nigel, M.A., Sc.D., b.1910. Educated Shrewsbury and Balliol. F.R.S., 1947. Member Advisory Council Scientific Research, 1949. C.B., 1952. M. 1st. Rebecca Downing, 1935; 2nd. Stella Vivien Norris, 1952. Publications: "Mesons in Modern Physics"; "Uses of Radio-active Sodium in Plastic Surgery". Address . . .' While I was reading this Read came in and said the two men Burgin and Piper had asked to see me again.

It wasn't a good time.

Burgin was a man in his mid-twenties, ugly and tall, with concave spectacles. Piper was older, square-shouldered, dark. I said: 'Mr. Read tells me you'd both like to become inspectors. Do you have any qualifications?'

Piper said: 'We've worked for five years with R.E.C. I was a general fitter and my mate did assemblies. Before that I was with Merlin Radio and Burgin was in the R.A.F. in a repair shop. There isn't much we don't know about our jobs, neither of us.'

I said: 'Of course you're both skilled men, I know that. But to be an inspector you have to be able to check and understand circuitry—and you have to have a certain amount of theoretical knowledge. If you could get your certificate I should be only too pleased to put you on to-day. As you can see, the shortage is holding us up.'

Burgin said: 'What do you do to get this certificate?'

I glanced at Read who was standing by the hygienic Crittall window with no expression at all on his cheerful, tough little mug. He didn't speak, so I went on: 'There's a man called Heaton in the shop—I don't know if you've met him yet—he's studying two nights a week. It's not really difficult—six or seven months at one of the night schools in Letherton or Chelmsford. As soon as he gets through he's sure of a job here. Why don't you do the same? It means an extra £4 a week.'

Piper said: 'Two nights a week for six months is a lot of time. You'd make a lot if you worked that much overtime.'

'Are the night schools free?' Burgin asked.

'No. There's a charge, but it's not a large one.'

'And who'd pay that?' said Piper.

'You would. Who else?'

He said: 'Well, it's to the advantage of the firm, isn't it? They need the inspectors.'

I said politely: 'We need inspectors but not that badly.'

A smile moved across Piper's face. He looked like a man who has just seen the catch in the three-card trick.

'Well, if that's the way it is, I reckon we'd best be going. Come on, Jack.'

But it was the wrong day for me. I said: 'Just a minute.'

Burgin, who had been about to follow Piper to the door, hesitated and Piper stopped.

I said gently: 'People like you make me want to fetch up. You think I'm the boss, and so I am. You may think I'm doing very well for myself, and so I am. But it happens to be a fact that before I started in this business I was poorer than you—quite a bit poorer. And I'm not talking of back in Victoria's time. I'm talking of seventeen and fourteen and even ten years ago. When I was in my teens and trying to mug up this sort of work I needed books—and not books out of a library but books to live with. So I did without my lunch every day so I could buy them. I went on doing that and things like it for several years. I'm not a very admirable person—far from it—and I don't ask you to copy me; but what success I've got I haven't had handed to me on a plate. I've had to make sacrifices for it—and I still am making them. If you're both so gutless that you expect the welfare state to pay for your night school, then I give you up and I hope the state will too.'

Piper said: 'We came here to ask a civil question. Perhaps it's too much to expect a civil answer, eh?'

Burgin put his hand on Piper's arm. 'Cut it out, Joe. This won't get us nowhere. Come on.'

Piper hesitated. I was tempted to say more but just held my tongue. He said: 'Well, thanks for nothing, mister.'

They went out. I leaned back and carefully lit a cigarette. Read detached himself from the radiator on which he'd been leaning and looked at the marks on his hands.

'Nice work, if I may say so, Mr. Granville. Turves like that.'

'I was a damned fool and lost my temper.'

'Perhaps it would be better if you did it more often.'

But it seemed to me that I'd only been putting into my dislike of them something of my dislike of myself.

At Greencroft there was still no letter from Lynn. I wondered what I should have felt if there'd been word from her that she was coming home to-morrow.

The house was cold in spite of the weather. I opened one or two windows and switched off the electric water-heater, which had been left on all the time. On a larder shelf some tomatoes had gone bad, and in the bread-bin were three half loaves green with mould. I threw them out.

Back in the drawing-room everything seemed dusty to the touch. I opened the gramophone and saw there were some records still on the turn-table, but I hadn't the interest to run them through. I tried the TV set and stared for a few minutes at a dull play about Florence Nightingale. I wasn't staying here to-night, but I felt I ought to see Mrs. Lloyd to see how Kent was going on. Then it suddenly occurred to me to wonder if at any time during the week-end Lynn had been for her key.

I opened the front door and looked under the plant pot. The key was still there. After a minute I realised that somebody was standing in the drive.

It was a middle-aged, loose-jointed man in a shiny blue suit and a trilby hat with a warped brim. He had a long horse face and he walked as if he was afraid of waking someone.

'Mr. Granville?'

'Yes?'

'Mr. Michael Henry Granville?'

I said I couldn't deny it.

'Then, sir, it's my duty to serve you with this petition.' He put a paper into my hand. 'Good evening to you, sir.'

He went off down the drive with his dormitory walk. I looked at the long envelope in my hand, and then stared after him until he disappeared. I opened the thing.

It was a petition filed by my wife. She claimed a divorce on the ground of my misconduct with Mrs. Stella Vivien Curtis, of Raglan Cottage, Letherton, Essex.

12

The girl took the pencil out of her mouth and put it in her red-gold hair.

'Yes, sir?'

The offices looked as if they had survived the Great Fire, but she wasn't of the same vintage.

I put the paper on the counter. 'This petition has been served on me by your firm. I'd like an interview with whichever of your principals was concerned in issuing it.' I looked at the glass door. 'Mr. Webber—or Mr. Sterne—or . . .'

She smiled slightly and re-stabbed with the pencil.

'They're both dead, sir. But I think it would be . . . Excuse me.' She went back into the cavern and whispered with a spectacled girl. 'Yes, sir, it would be Mr. Shelley. Do you want to see him?'

'I do.'

She went to the phone and came back with a doubtful expression on her young face.

'What name is it, please?'

'Granville.'

'Yes—er—Mr. Shelley's engaged. Would you wait?'

I waited. It felt about an hour before I was shown in.

Mr. Shelley didn't look like a poet. He was a fat man with eyes almost closed and huge pouches under them like ladies' handbags.

'Mr. Granville? How d'you do. You wished to see me?'

I handed him the petition. 'You are acting for my wife in this?'

'We are.'

'And on her authority?'

'Naturally. On her affidavit.'

'So she approves of this very strange document?'

He opened his eyes sufficiently to look at his finger-nails. 'Frankly, Mr. Granville, I'm not really in order in seeing you at all. But I thought as you had called perhaps there was some specific point. . . . Obviously I can't discuss the nature of the evidence with you. You should go to your own solicitor.'

'Would you tell me one thing?'

'If I can.'

'How long have you been having me watched?'

He put on a pair of library spectacles and turned the petition round as if it had been in a fever hospital. 'The first evidence is on May the 26th.'

'That wasn't what I asked you.'

'It's all I can tell you.'

'I suppose this petition can still be withdrawn?'

'Er—yes. It can be withdrawn at the instance of your wife.'

'So the best thing is to go and see her?'

His chair creaked as he shifted his weight. 'The courts are naturally always glad to encourage reconciliation.'

'Where can I find her at present?'

'It's on the petition.'

'That's only an accommodation address.'

'I think you can get in touch with her there.'

I stared at him for a minute. He pushed himself slowly out of the chair and walked ponderously across the room with his thumbs in his waistcoat pockets.

'If I may advise you on one thing, I should certainly go and consult a solicitor first. Put all the facts before him and then do what he suggests.'

'How long have I before I must reply to this thing?'

'You have eight days to "enter an appearance" as it's called. You file an answer denying the charge—that's if you wish to deny it. Then in three or four months the case will come into court.'

'Are you my wife's usual solicitor? Have you ever acted for her before?'

He didn't like that. 'We've not acted for her before. Many women don't have occasion to use a solicitor until something like this crops up in their lives.'

Grosvenor Court Mews was not quite where I'd pictured it, but I found it after a couple of false starts. It was one of those quiet backwaters that you find in Mayfair: a rectangle of cobbled and paved yard in which someone always seems to be washing down a Rolls-Royce, two or three tiny houses, made up out of old servants' quarters and painted in over-bright yellows and blues, a few garages and flats over.

No. 9a was one of the flats over. I went up the stairs and rang the bell. No answer. From what Ray had said I had hardly expected it. Yet she might have come back.

I lifted a gnome's head on the door and let it fall. There was no outside handle to the door but I pressed it just in case. It was locked. At a branch in the stairs just below was a door marked 9, so I went down and put a finger on that bell.

A dog yapped sharply, and after a bit there were footsteps and the door was opened by a small, elderly, spectacled woman with grey, shingled hair and a black velvet head-band. She was carrying a toy dog so overgrown with hair that it seemed to have no face at all.

I said: 'I beg your pardon. Does Mrs. Granville live here?'

'No, she lives at 9a, at the top of the stairs, but she's not at home.' The voice wasn't a bit friendly.

'Do you know when she'll be back?'

The woman shook her head emphatically. 'No idea at all. She's changed her habits these last weeks. Pepe, darling, don't go sleep. Just when Mother's cooked somet'ing 'licious for you.'

I stared at the dog. Now it had stopped yapping you could practically only tell which was the front end by the tip of red tongue that occasionally came out and licked what your sense of decency presumed to be its nose.

I said suddenly: 'These last weeks? But surely Mrs. Granville has only had this flat a very short time?'

'Not by my way of reckoning. She's had it since March Quarter Day, and she rents it from me.'

I stared at her and she blinked back at me.

'Thank you.'

'You're welcome.' Muttering to the dog, she'd already turned away, and the door was closing.

I said: 'Do you happen to remember when Mrs. Granville was here last?'

'Remember?' The woman didn't raise her head, and, staring at the grey hair, I suddenly saw a likeness between her and her dog. 'No, I don't remember. I'm in and out myself all day and I don't keep watch on my tenants.'

'No, of course not——'

'She was upstairs last Thursday night, but she came in so late I didn't see her. She's always here Thursday to pay the rent. She a friend of yours?'

I hesitated. 'Yes.'

It was the wrong answer. 'Well, then you'll know.'

I said: 'Is it usually late on a Thursday when she comes in?'

She closed the door another inch. 'Yes. Too late. That is since the time when she used to be here in the afternoons. I've got to go now. My kettle's boiling.'

'Thank you for helping,' I said, 'Mrs,—er——'

'Miss,' she said. 'Miss Lord.' And shut the door.

There was a phone box in the corner of the mews, and I rang Simon Heppelwhite for Hazel Boylon's address. He gave it me and I went out to Swiss Cottage. Simon said Hazel was working for a film company, so it wasn't likely I should find her in. But I thought there was a reasonable prospect of catching Lynn. As I climbed to the third floor of the Victorian house where the flat was, my heart was beating with more than the effort of climbing fifty-four stairs.

There was no bell, and no one answered the knocker. Then after a second try I could hear someone moving in the flat.

It was three weeks to-morrow. I wondered in what way she would have changed—whether sight of her would sweep away Stella and the thing of Sunday, whether——

The door opened. It was Hazel Boylon, in a flowered green house-coat. Her hair was tied back in a horse's tail with a piece of green lace, and there was lipstick on her teeth.

'Yes?' she said, and then: 'Oh, it's Mike.'

'How are you? Is Lynn here?'

'Lynn? No, dear. Did you expect her to be?'

I followed her in. It was a big, high bed-sitting-room, done in ivory and peach, both rather faded. The bed wasn't yet pushed up into the wall.

'Sorry, dear. I was washing some nylons. Hence the shambles. There are cigarettes somewhere—oh, here. Can you find a landing strip—shift those magazines.'

I shifted the magazines. 'I hoped I might catch Lynn. I wasn't dead-sure whether she was still with you.'

She was looking at her finger-tips. 'Washing plays hell with one's varnish. What d'you mean, still with me?'

90

'Well, she's been staying here, hasn't she? I understood so.'

'No, dear. Not since that week-end in January. I haven't seen much of Lynn for a long time. She's had other fish to fry. . . . No, thanks, I've got a lighter here—if the damn' thing'll work. . . . You having squaw trouble, Mike?'

'You knew of it?'

'No, but when men come searching for their wives at midday with that needled look . . .'

'A man said Lynn had phoned him from your flat. Perhaps I misunderstood him.'

'You must have.'

'You haven't seen anything of her recently, then?'

'Not a sight. Oh, use anything for an ash-tray. Actually I've been busy myself until two weeks ago. I'm stand-in for Jennifer Kaplan, you know; but she's finished her picture, and when she rests I rest.'

'It must be an interesting life.'

'It's all right. But there's too much having the tip of your nose measured. Mike——'

'Yes?'

'Oh, nothing.'

I said: 'What did you mean by saying Lynn had other fish to fry?'

'It was just a saying. Don't you really know where she's gone?'

I said: 'I haven't an idea now.'

From the end of the street I telephoned Ray French. There was no reply from his flat but I caught him at the music publishers.

He said: 'No, I didn't actually speak to Lynn, old boy. In fact I didn't know she'd rung me till the following day when she dropped me the briefest note. It was about the gramo-phone records, telling me to cancel them. That was all.'

'Can you remember just what she said?'

'I think I still have the card somewhere, but it's at home. It simply said: "Tried to get you on the phone yesterday, but no luck." Something like that. Then it went on about the records and it ended: "Am staying a few days with Hazel." '

'She actually put that?'

'Yes. Of course I don't remember *au pied*. The address was something like Scarsdale Mansions. Or was it Scaris-brook?'

'Scarsdale,' I said. 'Thanks.'

He said: 'Mike.'

'Yes?'

'W. Day has been brought forward a week.'

'What has?'

'Our wedding. It's fixed for the ninth, next Sunday, so we can catch the *Otrantes* which is leaving for a cruise on the tenth. As I said, it's not going to be a mammoth wedding, but we'd like you and Lynn.'

'Thank you. If you really want us both it might be a good idea to send separate invitations.'

'Oh? . . . Oh, I'm sorry if it's that way, Mike.'

'It's that way.'

'I'm sorry. What made you—but I suppose that isn't my business.'

'I didn't. She did.'

'Grave mistake on her part, I think. . . . Where do I find her?'

'I'll try to let you know.'

Whitehouse, of Tranter, Page and Whitehouse of Chancery Lane, was a big blond man in his early forties, round-faced, shock-haired, with nicotine stains on his fingers. I handed him the petition and he said: 'Oh, dear, I'm sorry about this,' and began to read it through. I thought, everybody seems to be sorry.

When he'd finished he flipped the thing with his finger and glanced at me. 'What's the answer? A denial?'

'Complete. The whole thing is nonsense.'

He drew a pad towards him and, tearing off a half scribbled sheet, began to make hieroglyphics on the new one.

'With an adultery charge the actual occasions need not be

specified on the petition—unlike cruelty where every detail goes down. "And on numerous other occasions between 27th May and 13th July." Can you remember what you were doing on those dates?'

'For the last two months I've been working very hard, so that one day has been much like another. My secretary might help.'

'This—er—Mrs. Curtis, who is in your laboratory—you were with her on those dates?'

'Probably. We were on a rush job and it meant long hours together.'

'And after hours?'

'Oh, yes. Often we worked late—and twice we had dinner sent in to us and went on afterwards, once until midnight.'

'You were quite alone in the factory then?'

'Yes—except for the two detectives who keep watch on the place during the night; and in that case I told them we were there and not to disturb us.'

'Did you work behind locked doors?'

'No.'

'Or with curtains drawn?'

'There are no curtains—but the windows of the laboratory are of reeded glass.'

'Did your wife complain to you of the association?'

'She complained about my working late—but not about Stella Curtis.'

'How did Mrs. Curtis go home afterwards? Had she a car?'

'No, I took her in mine.'

'Did you ever stop on the way?'

'Not as far as I can remember. Certainly not in any dark lanes.'

'And when she got home? Did you ever go in?'

'I'm not dead-certain whether I went in between those dates. I've been in quite a lot since. But her husband is ill and is always in the house.'

'Bedridden?'

'Not exactly.'

'Would he be upstairs or down when you went in?'

'Down. Except for once later when I went up to see him.'

'Has he ever shown any resentment at your association with his wife?'

'None at all.' Too little, poor devil.

'Have you taken Mrs. Curtis out in any other way—on any social occasion?'

'No. I had to take her to Harwell once and I took her to my own home twice.'

'Your wife would be at home, I suppose?'

'No.'

'Can you give me the details?'

'The first time was on the way back to the factory from Harwell. I wanted to pick up some plans so I called in and got them. That would be about half-past twelve midday—and I was there probably thirty-five minutes. The second——'

'Just a moment. Was there anyone in the house at all?'

'Our daily woman was there when we got there, but she left soon after we arrived.'

'Was it natural for her to leave then?'

'Yes. As a matter of fact I was surprised to find her still there, as she usually left at twelve when my wife spent the day in London.'

'Did you express surprise to the daily woman that she was still there?'

'I really can't remember.'

Whitehouse's pad was now well covered with doodles. He tore it off and began again.

'And the second time?'

'I had to go back home because I'd forgotten some notes I'd made overnight, and since there was a panic on that day I took Stella Curtis along with me so that we could continue talking in the car.'

'What time of day would that be?'

'About the same.'

'Was your wife——?'

'No, it happened to be Wednesday again. And this time

94

Mrs. Lloyd wasn't there either. But we only stayed ten minutes.'

He was staring at the end of his pencil. I wondered if he was really thinking of my problems or only shadow boxing.

He said: 'You can't think of any occasion when perhaps some casual intimacy occurred—the way things do sometimes nowadays—which would be taken the wrong way by anyone paid to watch you. . . .'

I said grimly: 'No intimacies, casual or otherwise.'

He nodded. 'Quite. I wasn't suggesting anything serious; but these days people do call each other darling and kiss each other on the shortest acquaintance.'

I said: 'She was my technical assistant. People don't kiss their laboratory assistants if they want to get any work done.' But what about when the work is finished!

'Or letters? Have you corresponded?'

'No.'

He put the pencil down and picked up another with a sharper point. 'What I'm driving at, Mr. Granville, is this. Obviously opportunity has existed in plenty. You could have been carrying on a fine affair with the young lady for all one can tell to the contrary. But evidence of opportunity alone is not sufficient to get a divorce. Otherwise no business executive out with his secretary would be safe. There must reasonably be some evidence to show infatuation or undue familiarity. Mind you, the opportunities in this case have been unusually varied—I'm looking at it from a legal point of view, you understand. But all the same'—he made several delicate figure eights on the pad—'if a woman came to me with no more evidence than this, I should tell her that she hadn't grounds for a divorce.'

I thought it out. 'This firm who are acting for her . . .'

'Yes, it's a point. In law of course there's no bar to a wife bringing a suit on the flimsiest grounds. The only real obstacle is that a solicitor of any repute won't waste his own time and his client's money.'

'And these people?'

He made a face. 'They're not tip-top. But I shouldn't

really have thought . . . I'll make some inquiries about them in the next few days.'

I got up. 'This suit's complicated for me in more ways than I've explained up to now.' I hesitated, and noticed what looked like a glint of speculation in his eyes. I suppose solicitors' clients often hold back their own confessions to the end. 'Mrs. Curtis's husband is a very sick man. I'm not certain if you'll have heard of John Curtis, but he's well known in the scientific world. He's very devoted to his wife, has complete trust in her. That's something I wouldn't willingly see lost.'

'Hm . . . It's a complication, I agree.'

'He's a man I've got a great respect for. To me he's—one of the exalted few. At this stage of the game there isn't much I wouldn't do to avoid poisoning his thoughts of his wife. . . .'

'Think Mrs. Granville knows that?'

'She certainly doesn't know how I feel about Curtis. But I've been wondering whether she's trying to use this threat of divorce as a lever. . . .'

He watched me. 'I don't think——'

'If my wife goes on with this thing, dragging Stella Curtis's name into it, I'll fight it all down the line. But if she really wants a divorce and is prepared to withdraw this petition . . . then I'd be willing to provide her with evidence that I wouldn't defend . . .'

Whitehouse frowned at me. 'Collusion is a bar to divorce. Mr. Granville——'

'It happens every day.'

'Quite. But it's not a thing I could knowingly be a party to.'

'Has my wife to appear before her solicitors in the near future?'

'There's no particular reason why she should. You mean because it might help you to trace her?'

'Yes.'

'Perhaps we could assist you over that. I'm not sure. In the meantime——'

'In the meantime,' I said, 'the main thing is to keep any knowledge of this trumped-up suit from John Curtis.'

'That may be difficult, Mr. Granville.'

'Why?'

'Well, in all probability by now his wife will have been served with a petition herself.'

13

When I got to the works about four, Read had the usual problems to be solved, and there was a pile of letters on my desk no higher than the typewriter.

I said: 'Has Mrs. Curtis come to-day?'

'Yes. She's in the model shop, I think.'

I breathed again. 'Tell her——'

'And Piper and Burgin have turned up too. I didn't expect them after the row yesterday. There's one other thing, Mr. Granville. A rumour's going round that McGowrie is a Communist.'

'Who?'

'The red-headed chap we've had about a fortnight. He came from British Electric.'

'Who told you?'

'It's the people working next to him who are complaining. They say he makes no secret of it, and they don't like it.'

'You'd better have him vetted,' I said. 'Put a call through to London at once. And Bill——'

'Yes?'

'I want a session with Mrs. Curtis now, so let me know the answer later on, will you?'

'Right.'

When he had gone I pressed the speaker and said to Miss Allen: 'I want Mrs. Curtis, please, and will you keep all phone calls out, and no tea till I ring.'

'Yes, sir.'

I thought, yes, even that's suspicious if it's a woman you're dealing with, and a dirty-minded private detective comes round making inquiries.

Stella came in. She didn't look well this afternoon and not as pretty as usual. But I knew the instant I saw her. It was a recognition of loving someone as involuntary as a reflex action.

I got her a chair. She said: 'Boss waits on lab assistant. It won't do, Mike.'

I could tell now by her manner that she hadn't yet had the petition, and her rather desperate flippancy gave me the chance to go right to the point. But I just couldn't throw it at her in the first second of meeting.

'How have things gone with you?'

'I'm all right.'

'And John?'

'I told him I was leaving here.'

'What did he say?'

'Didn't altogether approve. He thinks this work keeps my brain occupied. He likes you, you know.'

I picked up a pencil and began to dab it at the desk. 'I'm a man on a skewer. Like that, and that, and that. . . .'

Her long, dark-blue eyes went slowly over my face. 'And the more you hate yourself, the more you hate me.'

'Stella, you know that isn't true.'

She got up and went to the window. 'One thing follows on the other, doesn't it? I didn't tell you what you should have known about John. If you *had* known, what happened probably wouldn't have happened. You thought of him as a—a middle-aged civil servant or something, ailing, anæmic, a bit of a crank. If you thought of him at all on Sunday you thought of him that way. Isn't it true?'

'I don't know. If——'

'And it made all the difference. Didn't it? Didn't it?'

'That hasn't any bearing——'

'So you've a fairly good excuse—that's if you feel you need one. I have not. I knew all about John. I knew of his distinction, his courage, his almost saintly acceptance of

98

this—this blasted thing that's come on him. I know it in a way that you'll never know. But it didn't count, did it? Give me a chance and I'm ready for any lark—a bit of a flirtation with the boss, whoops, it's more than that, what a good job we've found a hut, *and* some dry sacking, never mind if it's dirty, this *is* fun, isn't it. . . .' She stopped, then turned away and went to the bookshelves with the scientific and trade magazines, picked one up, looked through it, put it down, came back to the desk.

'Mind if I have a cigarette?'

I handed her the box and she took one and I lit it for her, wanting so much to touch her. She drew at it once or twice, holding it uncertainly between lips and fingers, then took it out, stared at the tip with its faint blue smoke spiral.

'Sorry, Mike. Sorry.'

'So you should be.'

'But it's *true*. One can so easily mock up excuses like those I made last night; but they don't really count at all.'

Silence fell for a minute or so. I said: 'I've got to tell you that something else has turned up, something—quite fantastic, and I honestly don't know how to begin.'

She looked at me again. 'About Lynn?'

'Yes. She's petitioning for divorce. On the grounds of my . . .'

I took the petition out and handed it to her.

While her colour was coming back I told her quietly what I'd done so far.

She said: 'But the whole thing—as it's put down here . . .'

'I know. A hatch of lies. Up to the time the petition speaks of—up to the thirteenth of July—I'd hardly consciously thought of you as a woman at all.'

'Thank you.' When I glanced at her she raised her eyebrows. 'No, I mean it.'

'The fact that since that time, since Lynn or some threadbare detective turned in this so-called evidence, we've made the substance of the case true, doesn't compel us to admit what didn't happen.'

'I'm thinking chiefly of John.'

'So am I—oddly enough and a little late in the day. But I don't feel a sham in denying this bogus stuff, Stella.'

'No. . . .'

'The point is to stop it before it gets anywhere.'

'Through Lynn?'

'Yes, through her, when I find her. And before that we must somehow make sure that John is nowhere about when you're served with this petition.'

There was silence for a while. I said: 'If it were not for John I wouldn't want to fight this at all.'

Her cigarette had mostly smouldered away. 'Wait till you've seen Lynn again.'

'Look,' I said, 'I don't know what's happened to me and I don't know why it's happened—all I know is that it has. Stella, look at me.'

She looked at me. Suddenly she gave a little shiver. 'All right, I take it back if you feel like that.'

'I do feel like that.'

'All right, then. . . . But it isn't going to make it any easier for me to stay here.'

'I think you must until this thing works itself out.'

'Why has Lynn brought this petition, Mike? It's such a back-door way out.'

I said: 'I'm coming to the conclusion I never really understood her. It's a pretty unpleasant reflection on the quality of my married life.'

'It doesn't follow that the fault has been yours.'

'If you can live with a woman for three years and at the end of it know as little about her and how her mind works as I apparently know about Lynn, then you can't be very intelligent or imaginative or sympathetic. And it can't make your expression of love for another woman very much to be prized or well regarded.'

'That rather depends on the woman.'

'It depends on her charity.'

'No,' Stella said. 'I think that's the wrong word.'

'Then——'

100

'Mike, it won't help now to try to find the right one.'

When she had gone I asked Miss Allen for my works diary. The 27th May, which was the first date, was the day of our visit to Harwell when I called back at our house for the plans of IDA for Frank Dawson. So I was being accused of committing adultery in my own home with a woman I then still called Mrs. Curtis. The 13th of July was the night I'd worked with Stella at the factory until after midnight.

Just then Read came in and said: 'Well, they've checked and wasted no time on it. McGowrie is an active member of the Communist Party. What do we do now?'

'Get him out.'

'How?'

'The way we did with Camley; reorganise the working arrangements and create a redundancy.'

'It won't be easy when we're so many under staff.' He hesitated. 'O.K. I'll fix it. But I doubt if we can do it by Saturday.'

'Make the best excuse you can. It doesn't matter much so long as it isn't the truth. Security won't want him here a minute longer than necessary.'

Just before it was time to break off, I went into the factory. As usual the main workshop had a rather echoing quietness about it, with people sitting and standing at their benches, but in the background was the muffled throbbing from the machine shop. It seemed as if I hadn't been in the place for weeks. I stopped and had a word with one or two of those who were on new work. I think they liked it but was never quite sure. I was never comfortable as the boss, and I sometimes wondered if they thought I was patronising them by chatting to them about things—like an M.P. being shown over. I didn't really know what they felt about me, yet I thought I ought to have done. It wasn't as if my upbringing had been materially different from theirs. I noticed McGowrie working away steadily, and saw that he was on a radar job that was fairly advanced but not exactly on the secret list. Piper didn't look up as I passed, but I caught the

101

glimmer of Burgin's spectacles and nodded to him. At least they hadn't walked out.

I exchanged a word or two with Heaton and decided that, such was the hold up, he must be made an inspector even before he'd got his certificate. I speculated on why the girls always had to go to the toilet in twos; did they find it embarrassing walking away on their own or did they go off merely for a gossip? I remembered what the Ladies had looked like when the factory was new: shiny and spotless and chromium and glass; and how it had looked the Sunday before last when I'd wandered in: a corner of the mirror cracked, the walls stained, a crushed lipstick on the floor.

It wasn't the night for overtime; we did that twice a week; a shortage of work-people suited those who were there because overtime meant a disproportionate rise in pay. Most of them were now quietly ending the day. The bell would go in ten minutes.

I waited till most of them had left and then picked up Stella and drove her home. We didn't speak for a time. She was sitting very much in her corner as if avoiding me. All it seemed to do was make me more aware of every movement and breath she took.

I said: 'If it's something you feel you can talk about, how did you first meet John?'

'He came over to see my chief at Oxford. We were carrying out some experiments he was interested in. I was there and we exchanged a few words; and the next day he wrote inviting me out to dinner.'

'He's much older than you?'

'Nineteen years. He was married before but his wife died. He has a son studying law in Canada. . . . We lived in Cambridge until this started. But when it did, he didn't want people always calling, so we moved. He's anxious to miss the publicity, to avoid being called a martyr to science, that sort of thing.'

'But you've no doubt that he is?'

She shook her head. 'No, I've personally no doubt at all.'

We turned into the main street.

She said: 'It's hard for you, who didn't know him, to imagine what he was like even twelve months ago.'

'You were happy?'

'Yes—we were happy.'

I said: 'Stella, one thing.'

'Yes?'

'You talk of his almost saintly acceptance of this thing. How do you feel? Can you accept it the way he does?'

'He hasn't ever expected me to. Perhaps he knows I'm too practical, too down to earth. Perhaps that's true of all women. I just see the personal tragedy for us, and the *waste*. I can't—relate it to any design. . . .'

Past the one set of traffic lights, past the Old Bull, the turning to the station.

We were only a minute from the cottage now.

She sighed deeply, with a catch in her breath. 'Oh, Mike, this is a mess, isn't it? If you're a long way from shore, how do you think I'm going on?'

'That's what I'm rather anxious to know.'

She said: 'I was trying to think of a verse all last night when I couldn't sleep but couldn't remember exactly. What is it? . . . Who swerve from innocence, who makes divorce, of something, something and a good name, recovers not his loss, but walks with shame, with doubt, with fear and haply with remorse. I can't think who wrote it, but he rather got my number.'

We stopped at the gate. There was no one in a shabby mackintosh lurking about.

'Can you come in just for a minute?'

I saw it was going to help her if she hadn't to go in alone, so I followed her up the path and she let herself in. John Curtis was down again and not looking quite so emaciated.

'Hullo, darling.' She kissed him. 'I brought Mike back for two minutes but he can't stay. You all right?'

'Better than last night. Employ your two minutes on a drink, Mike. Trouble is with these slight temperatures, one gets so thirsty, and alcohol is not encouraged. You're in good time to-night, my dear.'

103

'Yes.' She took off her jacket, and I watched the slip and flow of her young body as she straightened by the window and dropped the coat away from her. 'Mike's getting indulgent.'

John raised his eyebrows quizzically. 'He looks worried. Don't say the scintillometer is getting you down at this stage.'

I didn't reply. He said: 'I suppose, knowing who I am, you've no objection to her telling me these things——'

'Oh, God, no!'

'I wondered——' He stopped. 'Oh, I forgot to tell you, Stella, there's a registered envelope for you on the bookcase. Over there. That's it. It came this morning, just after you'd left.'

He went on talking and I watched her go slowly across to it. I watched her with the fascination of someone in a nightmare seeing an approaching calamity he can do nothing to stop. Whitehouse hadn't warned me that petitions could be sent by registered post. But I knew what it was the instant she picked it up.

14

Her finger went under the flap and broke the seal. Not suspecting, with a lifted eyebrow, she put her finger in and began to take out the paper.

As she did so I butted in in mid-sentence. 'John, I *am* worried—and for a special reason. I've got something to tell you that you won't much like, and that's why I came in this evening.'

He'd stopped and was watching me with his alert eyes. But the tone of my voice told Stella at once what she hadn't known before, and she stopped and held the papers unlooked-at in her hand.

In a cold sweat I said: 'You knew my wife had left me, didn't you?'

'Stella said something about it. But I got the impression she didn't know much herself.'

'Lynn and I didn't quite hit it off; she made it fairly plain she was tired of the way we lived, and three weeks ago she left me. That I thought was all. To-day—or rather last night—I had a nasty shock. I discovered that she has been having me watched for nearly three months. I've discovered it because she's had a divorce petition served on me. It absolutely floored me when it came. And the name of the woman she cites in this petition as having been—as being the woman I have . . .'

I stuck there and I saw his eyes change. He looked at Stella. 'Not you?'

Her head came up and she looked back at him, not flinching or moving at all. Before she could speak I said: 'Yes. I'll never forgive Lynn for this. Of course, it's a completely phoney trumped-up charge—as I don't think I need to tell you.'

After a second or so he glanced down and took out his pouch. He looked for his pipe and found it on the table beside him. With his long thin hands he began to roll some tobacco into a ball.

'No,' he said. 'I don't think you need to tell me.'

I didn't dare to look at her now. She said slowly: 'Is this thing—the petition?'

'I don't know. It may be.'

There was a crackle of the paper as she began to unfold it.

'I can't say what hell this is to me, to bring this extra trouble on you both. When I do find her, which should be soon, I'll do everything I can to get her to play this thing straight.'

He pressed the tobacco down in the bowl. 'Presumably she wants her divorce; and it may be important to her to be considered the innocent party.'

'If she wants the divorce, then I'll give her material for a divorce, but not this way.'

After that nobody spoke for a bit, because no one knew what to say next.

'Yes, this is it,' Stella said, and put the papers down on the table in front of John. He made no move to look at them.

She said to him: 'You know, there *isn't* a word of truth in this paper, darling.'

He looked up at her, and smiled. 'Have I looked as if I thought there was?'

'No, but so far you've only heard it from Mike. I wanted you to hear it from me.'

He patted her hand. 'If I didn't trust you I shouldn't trust myself.'

There was another deadly hold-up, which I broke as soon as I could think of words that would link together.

Stella quietly poured me a drink and brought it to me. She asked John but he shook his head. While we were talking she picked up the petition again and looked through it. The light from the window fell on her pale eyelids and the long dark glistening lashes. Presently she dropped the thing down and went out of the room.

I was thankful that I'd come in with her; but now that I was here I couldn't leave. After a while he asked me some question about Lynn.

I said abruptly: 'I've never been more conscious than I am at this moment of the complete crack-up of everything in my life that up to now I've tried to persuade myself was worth while.'

'If as you say you were fond of her——'

'No, it isn't just that. . . . I should have *known*, I feel that I've been too damned obtuse to have a notion of what she's been feeling and thinking for months. For that and for other reasons I find it quite hard to live with myself. Everything I've *done*, it seems to me, bears out your judgment of the type of man you told me I was.'

'Hold hard. I hope I wasn't judging anybody.'

'I don't know if life generally is a sordid and nauseating mistake, but mine certainly seems to have become just that. The intelligent ape; isn't that it? Full of ingenuity and technical tricks——'

'Sit down,' he said, 'and don't talk nonsense.'

'The nonsense was yours, and it makes good sense to me at the moment. But I don't quite see your solution as a thing that would be a solution for me.'

'My solution? What is it? Having some belief in the spiritual dignity of man? I don't know that it's a hold-all for everybody's perplexities. I don't find it much more than adequate at times.'

'But adequate.'

He smiled. 'Perhaps one of the more unagreeable truths is that man is born with a debt that for a time he isn't aware of owing. But all the time it piles up; and somewhere, usually in his middle years, life suddenly and unscrupulously presents him with an account rendered. Then it depends on the quality of the man, how and whether he tries to pay.'

There was a long silence. I said: 'You've taken this petition, this—this eruption into your private life—which must become harder to take every second you think of it—without a complaint, without a question. I'm—more than grateful to you for that.'

'Well . . . we're all in the mess together, aren't we?'

'Thank you for saying so.'

'Shut the window, will you, Mike? The evening's turning chilly for my thin blood. . . . You'll stay to supper?'

'I'd like to.'

When I came back from the window he had picked up the petition envelope and was looking at the address but making no attempt to open it. I said suddenly: 'John, tell me how you would feel in my place—or no, not that. Tell me how you'd feel yourself if—if Stella, for instance, had come in with me to-night and said that the things in this petition were true.'

He got up slowly, moved to the fireplace.

'That's two questions, isn't it—what I'd do in your case and what I'd do in my own.'

'What you'd do in your own.'

'. . . I'm not at all sure. But being in the shape I am, I think I'd take steps to remove myself from the scene.'

'Completely from the scene?'

'Yes. It's a thing a reasonable man may choose to do in certain cases, even though it's not to be approved of generally. There's a gas fire in the next room. The gas is non-poisonous, but it's inflammable and one could make a bang. I think it would appeal to my sense of humour, that way out. The *reductio ad absurdum* of atomic physics—the Victorian gas fire and the lighted match.'

'Perhaps it's the recipe for me.'

'No, not for you. You've still plenty of time to pay.'

When I left, which I did about nine, I drove into London to see Lynn's mother again. But she didn't seem able to help. The few hints and addresses I got smelt like old trails. I booked a room at a hotel in Piccadilly, garaged my car, and walked up to Grosvenor Court Mews. The time was just on midnight and there was a light in Miss Lord's flat but none in the one above. There were two windows of No. 9a flat looking out over the mews.

At half-past twelve the lights went out in No. 9. I waited a long time. A policeman glanced at me a couple of times but didn't tell me to move on. At two I went back to the hotel. Evidently Lynn wasn't coming to-night. But to-night was Wednesday. Miss Lord said it was Thursdays she came to pay her rent.

By lunch-time next day, having drawn blank on Mrs. Carson's trails, I rang the works and found that Frank Dawson was back from Llanveryan.

He said: 'Only here for the day, Mike. Is it all *right* for me to go back to-morrow? I'm not a lot of use, but they seem to like someone on the spot.'

'Yes, that's O.K.'

'You'll be in at the works to-day?'

Something in his voice. 'I'm not sure. Why?'

'Well, Read's having a bit of trouble. I think he's gone a step too far this time.'

'What is it?' I asked irritably.

'Apparently he's sacked somebody, one of the electricians,

and there's a hoo-ha because he's a Communist.'

'We checked up. I told Read to get rid of him. But I presume nobody's been fool enough to say why.'

'Maybe Read's been incautious. Anyway, it's got out and some of the men are pretty het-up.'

I said: 'Put me on to Read.'

'O.K. I will. How's Lynn?'

I hesitated. Had he heard too? 'She was all right the last time I saw her. Fine.'

'Give her my regards. Hold on. I'm putting you through now.'

It took a few seconds and then I heard Read's voice. 'Hello, Mr. Granville. I suppose the sheep's been bleating his head off.'

'Is it true?'

'Afraid so. It may all blow over, but it's this damned principle of no victimisation. One or two of the fellows are looking ugly.'

'How did it get out?'

'It didn't so far as I know. McGowrie himself took it quite well. I had him in and told him and he said, "Is it because I'm a Communist?" and I looked surprised and said, "Not at all, it's just a reorganisation of the work." Then he went off and I heard nothing until about an hour ago, when one or two hotheads——'

'Who chiefly?'

'Piper.'

'Ah, I thought as much. And Burgin?'

'No, he doesn't appear to be taking any active part, at any rate.'

I thought a minute.

'Look, Read, take it easy. We don't want to fall down on delivery dates again—for R.R.E. this time. If we do we shall all be out of a job. Let the thing ride if you can, and for God's sake don't make an issue of it.'

'Right. But McGowrie must go?'

'Well, yes, there's no other way, is there. But most of the fellows are reasonable enough. They know as well as we do we can't have Commies on secret jobs. I wish Piper would fall in front of a lorry.'

'Will you be in to-day?' The same old question.

'I'm not sure. I'll try.'

Part of the afternoon I spent with Whitehouse again. Once the machinery had been put in motion, there was no real urgency from a legal point of view.

Feeling better because this at least was being taken care of, I came out and got in my car. It was half-past four. The fine weather of the last two weeks was breaking up, and heavy yellow clouds hung over the city. There was no air in Chancery Lane. To-night being Thursday, there was an obvious date to be kept with Lynn at No. 9a Grosvenor Court Mews. Nothing must interfere with that.

One or two spots of rain fell on the bonnet, spilt stars drying at the edges. A 67 bus ground past, followed by a wake of taxis and private cars. I thought, if the electricians came out at this particular stage and the Harwell thing is shot down by Steel ... In spite of high hopes my financial position was finely balanced, and I hadn't made things easier by not going after commercial contracts. I'd a very heavy mortgage on the new factory and had not yet sold the old premises. If everything was brought to a standstill now it would probably never re-start.

But it would take more than an hour to get to Letherton at this time of the day. By six everyone would be gone. Better to go straight to Hockbridge, pick up any letters, then go on to Letherton and call on Stella and John as I'd promised. She could tell me what was happening at the works. I realised that the need to see Stella, great as it had been all week, was each day an increasing one. Life wasn't going to be made any easier by that fact.

I drove down to Hockbridge.

Because of being served with the petition, I hadn't called on Mrs. Lloyd on Tuesday, so I went in there first. Kent greeted me with even more than his usual extravagant affection, knocking over a stool to get at me and nearly putting me on my back.

Mrs. Lloyd said she was going on quite well, but she'd be glad to know when Mrs. Granville was coming back because she didn't like being paid for nothing and she didn't have a key and the house would be getting dirty and neglected, and could I ask Mrs. Granville about the groceries when I wrote; and the gardener was asking when he came on Tuesday, and Mr. Lloyd was awfully fond of Kent but he said he was that much too big for a cottage.

I was fairly sure by now that Mrs. Lloyd had a good idea what was going on, even if she hadn't known from the start. Not much escaped *her* eyes. I told her I'd make arrangements about Kent if my wife wasn't back in another week, and in the meantime she wasn't to worry about the house.

I took Kent up to the house with me, as he looked as if he needed exercise, and he bounded ahead in an ungainly gallop, his white tail dipping madly. He would have to be sold or given away. I felt upset at the thought of parting with him, but I certainly had no intention of going on living here alone. The Old Bull at Letherton would have to be my home for the next few months.

The sky was still heavy but a more general grey than in central London, and the house was dark when I went in. There was a splay of letters, and I took them into the living-room to read them. There are few places more depressing than a house that's not being lived in, and I opened the french windows and stood on the top step looking out over the garden.

Nothing in Lynn's writing. A surtax demand I hadn't expected, an account rendered for some provisions, the electricity bill, a postcard for Lynn from some people in the South of France, a letter for Lynn which after a moment's hesitation I opened and found to be from the secretary of the local British Legion.

That was the lot. She was evidently going to play out this farce to the bitter end.

There was a flicker of lightning over the trees, and I waited for the rumble of thunder. It came at last, so distant that if I hadn't been expecting it I might not have noticed it at all. I wondered what had happened to Kent and then heard him in the hall.

The garden was getting in a mess. Smith had been ill; and then two days a week was not really enough at this time of year. The grass was long and going brown in patches. A downpour would do it all the good in the world.

There was another flicker of lightning, even more unimpressive than the first, but the thunder was nearer. Remembering that Kent was inclined to be frightened by storms I went to find him.

He wasn't in the hall but in the short dark passage to the kitchen. Here a door led down to the cellar, and he was scratching at that. I wondered if he was trying to get away from the storm, so I opened the door and he immediately scuttled in.

I went into the kitchen and wondered why kitchens always come to look neglected quicker than any other room in a house. The water in the sink usually accumulates enough to smell sour, and there's always grease on the stove or stale crumbs somewhere. I was going into the larder, but heard Kent barking excitedly, the way he did when he was enjoying himself, so I went back to the cellar steps.

There was only one main cellar really, a square room we used for junk, with two smaller places leading off, one for wine and one for coal. I switched on the light and went down.

Everything down here, at least all the rubbish in this middle cellar, would be a legacy for the new owners. There wasn't a thing of value—an old bedstead, some packing-cases, a table with a broken leg, spare rolls of wallpaper, some buckets and cleaning things. The bedstead *we'd* inherited. Kent was in the coal cellar, scratching at the anthracite, ears cocked and tail wagging in brief interested bursts. We hadn't paid for the anthracite yet. We'd be getting an account rendered for that.

Unfortunately, the only light was the one in the main cellar, and it was shadowy and dark where he was scratching at the great pile. The small stuff was constantly rattling as he brought it rolling down. I saw he'd got something greyish white almost under his paws, but it seemed to be part of a longer thing becoming outlined as the coal rolled away.

I said sharply: 'Come away, Kent; come away! What the hell are you doing?'

At the tone of my voice he stopped, head on one side, staring at me with his idiotic white face, then he yelped excitedly and went back to his scrabbling. Suddenly I kicked at him, and the tone of his yelping changed as he jumped away. The thing he had unearthed appeared to be a human hand and arm.

Still uncertain, I went a step closer. It was the right shape but the wrong colour and was part of a dummy or something, being a sort of red-brown in colour under the fine film of coal dust. I bent and caught hold of it to lift it out. The skin crinkled and pulled away under my fingers, and one enamelled red finger-nail came away in my grasp.

I started back with a gulp that choked me. Doing so I thrust away a pile of anthracite with my boots and all the surface began to move. Like a black tide it rattled down, partly covering the hand and arm but revealing farther up the face and head. It was almost unrecognisable, the skin copper-coloured like the arm, but with greenish blotches, the eyes black and sunk deep into the head, a stain of wet blood at the corner of the pinched and shrunken mouth. The flaxen hair, stained and contaminated by coal, appeared to be coming out. But I had no difficulty in recognising that, nor the single turquoise ear-ring in a darkly mottled ear.

I had found Lynn at last.

15

I was on the kitchen floor. I didn't know how long I'd been lying there. I remembered vaguely crawling on all fours nightmarish out of the dark pit, endless steps, with fright and sickness clutching at my bowels. The floor of the kitchen was stone, and my head lay just off the matting; the cold stone must have gradually brought me round.

On hands and knees again, I tried to vomit several times, then got to the sink and was really sick. I turned on the cold tap and shoved my trembling hands under it and splashed the water over my head and neck. After a bit the awful throbbing in my throat seemed to quieten, the blood to go out of my eyes. I straightened up and lurched sweatily out of the kitchen, past the hole from hell, across the hall, reached the drawing-room. The french windows were still open, and another flicker of lightning moved behind the trees.

I got as far as the desk where the drink was kept and took out brandy, couldn't see a glass, gulped three or four times at the bottle. The spirit went down hotly, was met first by another violent urge to be sick, but I flopped in a chair, fought it and fought it.

I lay there for a long time meeting the horror that kept getting at me. I was now just one step away from complete break up, but I couldn't get any farther.

It was a queer light in the room, not dark but not anything else, a false twilight because of the thunder-clouds. There was still really a couple of hours of day left, but I couldn't shake free from the idea that the light was fading. I knew I couldn't be alone there in the dark. I kept rubbing my fingers up and down on the settee to get the feel of her off them.

Then I saw the telephone at my elbow. I lifted it off. We weren't on a dialling system and I could hear the thing buzzing at the other end. They were a long time; just too long. The exchange girl said: 'Number, please,' but abruptly I put the phone back.

Because I had remembered Kent.

I took another gulp of brandy, gathering my strength. Then I got up and lurched back into the hall. It was darker here and less far from the cellar.

'Kent!' I shouted.

I thought my voice echoed as if the house was empty of furniture, as if it was empty of everything except my wife and the smell of her. I licked my lips and shouted again. Then he answered in a queer excited half-whine, half-bark from the cellar.

I got myself somehow to go step by step to the door. The light was still on but I couldn't see him down there. For a minute I just hadn't the guts to shout again because I thought if I did perhaps Lynn would get up, shaking the coal dust off her.

I went down a step. 'Kent!'

He barked but didn't appear. A few bits of anthracite rattled.

Then I lost my head and my temper. 'Kent, you damned bloody fool!' I screamed. 'Come out!' I listened to my voice as if it was someone else's and marvelled that it should be so hysterical. I cursed at him and swore. Then I turned to go. I must get help of some sort. To hell with the dog. I must get the police. That first impulse had been the right one.

But they might be ages coming. I couldn't *leave* him down there, with *her*, pulling at the coal and making his idiot whining. Besides I didn't know what he might be *doing*. I went down two more steps. From here I could just see the edge of the coal. I *couldn't* go any farther, not if my soul depended on it. I whispered 'Kent!' and suddenly he came, his tail wagging and his tongue lolling, grinning at me as if proud of his find, and then turned to go back to it. I fell down four more steps, grabbed at his collar, missed, clutched his haunches; my sweaty fingers slipped, I caught his tail, hauled him back, got at last a grip on his collar, trying not to look, trying not to see into the coal cellar; I turned and hauled him choking to the top of the steps. He was a heavy dog but I lifted him as if he was nothing. But I'd seen it again, out of the corner of my eye. I flung him slithering into the kitchen and slammed shut the cellar door and lay back against it, sweat running down me like rain. Then before he could come out I slammed the kitchen door also and knew he was safe.

As I stood there taking deep breaths, trying to steady up, the telephone in the drawing-room rang.

I got across to it, took another gulp of brandy, picked it up.

'Hullo.'

'Mr. Granville?'

'Yes.'

'Oh, this is Frank Dawson. A bit of luck catching you, Mike. I thought I'd try the number to see if you were there.'

'Yes.' Tell *him*? Ask *him* to get help?

'I thought you'd want to know the latest about the works dispute. Piper has called a strike for to-morrow morning.'

'Oh.'

'Hullo.'

'Hullo.'

'I say Piper has called a strike for to-morrow morning.'

'Yes.'

'I think Read has mismanaged the thing from the start, don't you?'

Lynn's dead, Frank, I would say. I've just found her. Somebody's *killed* her. No, in this house, in the cellar. And I took her hand, Frank. The wedding ring was on it. . . .

'Of course, Gill is shop steward, and it's not Piper's place to take the lead, but he seems to be one of those men who can get away with it. I told you I was going back to Wales in the morning, didn't I?'

'Oh.'

'Are you all right?' What, Lynn dead? Are you joking man? When? Where? Incredulous, he would be; incredulous, suspicious, staring.

'What?'

'I say, are you all right?'

'Yes . . . I'm . . .'

'I thought you sounded a bit queer. Is Lynn at home?'

Is she at home? Yes, come over, Frank, and meet her. I said: '*Why?*'

'Oh, I just thought I'd like to hear the sound of her voice.'

I glanced round, thinking I heard the sound of her voice.

'No, she's not at home.'

And then he rang off. The chance was gone. I suddenly felt that by saying nothing to him I'd done something not revocable. Yet far better to get help direct. Handle this on my own. Fumble a cigarette out of the box on the table and light it. Take up the telephone again.

And then again I put it back. Perhaps there had been something un-revocable *within my own mind* in not telling Frank Dawson. At least the thought of Frank, incredulous, unbelieving . . . Other people would be just as incredulous, just as likely to see this, inconveniently, through their own eyes, not through mine. Among them the police. What would *you* think if you were a policeman? Go slow.

One of the french windows started to swing, and I jumped in the chair as if I'd been shot. I thought someone was shutting me in. But it was only a stray breeze.

I knew I'd got to think, and think more clearly than ever before in my life. But not in this house. I couldn't *stay* in here because if I did, not one straight thought would come. You couldn't while that lay in the coal cellar. I could still follow first impulses, ring for the police or for help of some sort. I knew it was best to do that. But I couldn't for the moment reason out the follow-on of making that move—or the consequences of not making it.

I went out of the french windows, down the steps into the garden. I got well away at the end of the lawn, flopped on a tree stump.

Lynn had been dead some time, and someone had killed her. People don't die, get themselves buried under anthracite.

But who? I was her husband. We'd not been getting on. She'd decided to divorce me, had cited another woman; I'd been furious, resentful at the idea of a divorce, had wanted to stop it. She'd refused; we'd quarrelled violently.

That was the lay-out. I tapped the end of the cigarette and tried to keep it still. It wouldn't keep still. I held it up and looked at it. It wouldn't keep still.

A car went past on the road that Lynn had used on the Friday night when she'd come back to fetch something. I'd run across this grass after her then, through the trees. She'd lost one ear-ring. Three weeks ago to-morrow. Why had she come back that night and when had she come back for the last time?

Who had last seen her? On the Saturday or Sunday after leaving me she'd replied to the bank's letter. Much later, nearly a week later than that, Ray French's postcard. Miss Lord had had the rent of her flat only six days ago.

But she hadn't seen her. She said Lynn had come too late. For that matter, neither had Ray, and the postcard had given wrong information.

I looked back at the house; it was dark and square-shouldered and baleful against the trees and the sky. Out here was some kind of sanity and safety. But whatever I thought up, I had to go in once more—either to phone the police or to fetch Kent and lock the door. A spot of rain was cold on my hand.

I swallowed; saliva was all the time gathering in my mouth, and three or four times I had spat it out. I needed more brandy, but that too was in the house. Not the courage to go back yet. Another cigarette.

Steady, think it over. Don't rush into a primary error. It could be as big a bloomer *not* to call the police as to call them, probably much greater. I didn't know. I'd *got* to know. A flash of lightning lit the sky, and I waited for the thunder. This time it never came.

It wasn't really any use trying to reason clearly even out here. Every now and then I'd think things were beginning to settle; but all the time I was doing it with the lid off. Nothing solidified, took shape. Nothing could.

The rain came faster. Must go back to the house. At this moment I had one advantage over everyone else. I only—apart from the murderer—knew I hadn't killed my wife. If the police were called in they'd automatically make me chief suspect. Could I turn this advantage to any gain before I reported the body? I thought, if I don't tell the police, can I

118

go about the ordinary business of living, without people knowing what I've seen—even for a few hours?

How did murderers manage to do it as if nothing were the matter? Did they have some inner skin to the mind which stopped them from remembering?

Reason it out. Lynn had been dead for some time. At first the sight of the wet blood had deceived me, but common sense insisted. . . . Who then went to her flat in Grosvenor Court Mews late at night? To-day was Thursday. Someone came on Thursday late to pay the rent. Presumably they slipped the money in an envelope into Miss Lord's letter-box. Something of that sort, to avoid a meeting or a cheque. How could anyone risk going to the flat unless they knew Lynn was dead?

I went back to the house.

Kent was quiet now. Nothing stirred or moved. I went upstairs. It was queer the feeling, as if going away from the doors of the house was moving away from safety. If Something followed up the stairs the retreat was cut off. I went into our bedroom. Although it wasn't really dark in here I put on the light. I went over to her dressing-table and began to search through the drawers.

The scent she used came from her things, and suddenly I had to stop because I found tears running down my face. Perhaps it was weak and shameful being like that, but the scent brought up all sorts of memories; it had been a part of the early days of our marriage in London with all the physical companionship of the long nights, the shared excitement, the comradeship, the sense of heightened living.

I sat there miserably for a time, not able to go on. And as I sat there my feeling for the thing in the cellar changed. I was still scared of it, in an illogical instinctive way, but a lot of the fear had given way to pity and anger. No doubt it was true that Lynn hadn't much liking for me before the end; but that didn't change what I felt and had felt about her. She was my wife, and someone had murdered her and dragged her down into the cellar, and left her alone in the dark and the dirt and the ignominy.

119

Kent was barking now, and with a sudden lurch of fear I went out to the landing window and peered down the drive. There was no one about. I went back to the bedroom.

A few old bills, two theatre programmes, a list of Festival Hall concerts, underclothes, handkerchiefs, shoes, folding coat-hangers, needles and silk cotton, an old handbag quite empty. Lynn had been a great spender, and there were about two dozen frocks hanging in the wardrobe. I should have realised she wouldn't have left so many of her things behind. I began to feel in the pockets of her day dresses, and immediately came on a note that was a shock. It was on a piece of the firm's notepaper and simply said: 'My dear Lynn, Shall be delighted to see you Wednesday. Do ring me if you want to make it earlier, Frank.' The other thing I found, in an inner pocket of her Burberry, was a Yale key. That might not have meant anything except for the label tied on which said '9a'.

I took Kent back to Mrs. Lloyd's, told her I'd see about getting him moved as soon as I could. I don't know if I still looked queer; anyway she always peered at you as if she thought you'd been up to something.

I drove shakily back into London. By the time I got there it was nearly half-past ten. I still felt sick; it kept coming in fresh waves every few minutes like when you have food poisoning. I went into a snack bar and drank two cups of black strong coffee and swallowed a few mouthfuls of a plate of bacon and eggs. I couldn't remember when I'd last eaten. Nobody here in London had changed as I had changed. The girl who served me had the mark of an old gland operation on her neck. 'Scrambled egg and mixed grill, two teas. Well, they *say* they're invisible but it all depends who's looking, don't it? Three cheese and tomato. Milk shake.' There were sweat stains on the other girl's overall. 'Two fish and chips. It don't seem decent, not ever to be left alone.' She sniggered. 'Makes you think. Sorry, sir, no poached eggs; scrambled or fried. . . .'

The food stuck in my chest. I got up and went out,

garaged the car, registered at the same hotel. Then I walked down Piccadilly.

When I got into Grosvenor Court Mews there was a chauffeur waiting by a car near one of the other flats, and two girls talking under a lamp who eyed me. There was also a light in No. 9.

I waited about twenty minutes and then began to feel conspicuous, so strolled off towards Curzon Street and walked along it as far as Park Lane. I wasn't far now from the tiny flat we'd first rented; every step in this part reminded me of Lynn. The sky was an odd colour; there were pink reflections from the ground upon the heavy under-tow of the clouds, and a giant rift in them stretched half-way to the City.

I looked at my watch. It was ten to twelve. I turned back.

Just short of the mews I stopped to light a cigarette and heard Big Ben through, then I felt the key again and walked on.

The car had gone, the girls had gone. There was only a dog there sniffing at an empty can; he raised his head at my footsteps and watched me until I was past. I got as far as the garage end where I had watched last night and looked across at the windows of No. 9. They were in darkness. Miss Lord had retired to rest. But now there was a light in the windows of No. 9a.

16

I dropped my cigarette and pressed it into the stones of the yard. I took the key out of my pocket and looked at it. I waited a minute, taking breaths. Then I went in.

There was a small light burning at the first turn of the stairs, right opposite Miss Lord's door. I went past that, stopping once when a stair creaked. Then I came opposite the door of No. 9a. No light was to be seen under it.

I wiped the sweat off my hands and very very slowly put the key against the jagged opening in the Yale lock. Sometimes almost at the first touch you can tell whether they fit or not. This key slid in like a sword into its sheath. I turned my fingers and the tumblers turned. I pressed on the door and it opened with a very slight creak.

Now you could see why no light showed. This was a tiny vestibule, five by five; a door led off to the right, probably into a bathroom, the door straight ahead into the living-room. A light showed under this. There was a handle, but above it was another Yale lock.

Usually a second such door would be left permanently with its catch back. At least it was worth trying. I took two steps and listened. There was no sound from inside. I put my fingers slowly round the knob and turned. When it had gone far enough I put the fingers of my other hand against the door and pressed. It gave and began to open. As the first split of light showed down the length of the door, the light went out.

I let go the handle slowly and leaned against the door. It swung wide, opening into a vacuum of darkness. Then I didn't make any further move. My ears are pretty keen, and I thought I should pick up some sound of movement or breathing. It didn't come.

You could make out the oblong of one of the windows. The white blind was drawn, but there was just enough light from the street lamp at the end of the mews to mark the rectangle. By it you could see the shoulder of a chair, the glass of a picture on the wall, the sloping edge of a lamp-shade, a more anonymous bulk in the middle of the room.

I reached my hand slowly into the room and felt up and down the wall, found the smooth metal of a switch, went to press it down. But it was already down. Farther along the wall, but there was nothing else. I clicked the switch up. Nothing.

Now it was a question of nerves. The longer we waited the less his advantage would be. But I should have phoned the police instead of this. I knew that now.

Somewhere, I think in the flat below, a clock chimed the quarter-hour. A car accelerated away, its exhaust higher than the dying rumble of the traffic. Quiet fell again. Then there was a baby crying, perhaps it was in the house opposite; it went on and on and then suddenly checked and was still. Mother had come. I could hear my own heart beating; it didn't seem fast but it was emphatic. I wondered how long I would have to wait.

A sound over to the right in the darkest part of the room, as if someone had disturbed something by the smallest move. I stepped back towards the first door, groped for the switch, put on the light in the vestibule, then lurched sharply into the living-room, veering left, seeking the shadows there.

Light flooded into the room through the gaping door. Settee, bookcase, television set, piano—something hit me across the head, a new light flashed; I fell across a chair clutching at a coat as it went past me; he shook free; as I rolled to the floor I clutched an ankle; he kicked himself clear, stumbling against the door—darkness fell on me and I lay on the floor holding my head as the outer door opened and slammed.

I got to my knees, forced myself up, stumbled across to the window, scratched the blind away; the mews was empty. I waited. Perhaps he had gone or there was another way out. A great lump on the back of my head; the room wasn't steady yet. But I had to keep watching in case.

I swore and blasphemed—taken in by the oldest trick—a bit of paper or something thrown across the room to give the impression he was on the opposite side. I'd walked practically into him, yet not a recognisable glimpse.

A movement at the end of the mews by the telephone-box was almost out of my range of vision: I let the blind fall and ran down the stairs. When I got out there was no one to be seen.

The blow hadn't broken the skin but my head was thumping. I stumbled back up the stairs and into the flat. By the light of the vestibule I saw the bulb of the standard lamp on the settee and put it back in its socket. Then I went back to the door and switched on.

A settee in figured brocade before a built-in electric fire, and an easy-chair to match drawn up beside the sham-walnut television set. On a bleached-wood half-moon table by the wall was a typewriter, and next to it was a desk with a mirror over. I went to it and dragged open the drawers.

Again that scent of Lynn's, so cloying, so familiar. Notepaper—it was queer how scent always clung to paper—a cheque-book, a rent receipt. I lifted off the cover of the typewriter but there was nothing in the machine. A newspaper on a chair, two weeks old, a pair of her shoes. Another door half-open led into a tiny bedroom with a window looking out on the roof of another flat.

Lynn's things here: nightdress in a case on the bed, dressing-gown behind the door, in a corner the suit-case she had taken when she left—her initials in blue on the side. It was half-full of things neatly packed, a hairbrush, face lotion, handkerchiefs, stockings and the rest. There was only one letter in the bottom, and it was from Messrs. Sterne, Webber and Webber, saying that the petition was now drawn up and inviting her to attend at their offices when the affidavit could be sworn before a neighbouring solicitor. Dated July 14, two days before she had left me.

In the drawers of the room were a few things of hers, all clean, nothing soiled. The wardrobe held two of her frocks, a light summer coat. A small wicker laundry basket was empty. At least it looked empty until I saw a bit of paper at the bottom caught in a cleft of broken cane, and eased it out. It was about half an inch by a quarter and was a recognisable piece of a cigar band. I put it away carefully in my wallet and turned to the waste-paper basket. Nothing in there.

Back through the living-room to the other door leading off the vestibule. A bathroom. Her toothbrush, some nail varnish, her soap, made with the same scent, as I knew. And then I saw something that really startled me. On the glass shelf beside the toothbrush was my toothpaste.

I remembered now I'd missed it on the morning after she left me and had had to use hers. The natural inference was that in packing her case to leave she had taken my toothpaste in mistake for her own. But as it happened the natural inference would be entirely wrong——

Someone knocked on the outer door. It was a sharp rap, and for a second or so my thoughts were stuck like sheep in a gate. I took a step to the door and then stopped. The nature of the knock was wrong. I went to the windows and lifted the blind an inch away. In the mews below was a Wolseley police car. Beside it a flat-capped policeman stood and stared up at my window.

I let the blind fall. The knock came again. Well, I could answer it, couldn't I?

I went into the bedroom. The window looked out over a flat roof, a drop of perhaps six feet. Where did the roof lead? If back to the mews, then madness to try it. But the thing ran in the opposite direction.

I heard a scraping at the outer door as if someone were trying keys. I slid the window up and climbed out on the sill. It was an easy drop and I landed on my toes, almost without a thud. I ran to the edge of the flat roof and found there was no way out here. I either had to go back or on and across the next roof, which sloped V-shaped to a central guttering. As I pulled myself up to it a police whistle sounded.

Perhaps it's natural to have that effect on a law-abiding citizen when he suddenly finds himself on the wrong side of the law. I slithered along the valley between the roofs, and at the end came up against the blank brick wall of a house.

I glanced back and saw a policeman silhouetted as he got out of the window. I began to climb the sloping roof, clawing at the tiles with one hand and at the wall of the house with the other. I reached the apex of the roof, let myself slide down the other side and came up with a jerk that broke a piece of the guttering. Below there was some sort of a small courtyard. I let go and landed on hands and knees. The man was following.

The courtyard was entirely enclosed, but there was a

125

house with french windows at the end, and one of the french windows was ajar. I ran towards it, slid through, pulled the window behind me, fumbling through curtains into a long dark room with a number of shining tables that refracted the light from a half-open door beyond. It looked like an expensive restaurant or the dining-room of a club.

I felt my way down it towards the open door and a mutter of voices. A card-room; two tables were being used. Eight men playing bridge, the room heavy with cigar smoke. I looked round the room I was in. This was the only door.

One of my hands was scraped, so I dug it in my pocket and walked slowly into the card-room and towards the door at the other end.

I've never known a longer walk in my life. The 'dummies' of both tables turned and stared; one of the men playing a hand lifted his head and looked at me with a sort of hypnotised interest.

After about half an hour I reached the other door, turned the handle, thought it was locked, and then found it opened inwards instead of outwards. I went through. No one had spoken.

There were stairs. I went down the stairs. At the bottom was a large tiled hall with a porter's box, but the porter had gone off duty. The first doors to the street were easy. The second lot were locked and it took me a minute to find out how the lock worked.

Outside the street was empty, and about fifty yards away was a taxi-rank. I went up to the taxi there and gave him the name of my hotel. No one had come out of the club by the time the taxi turned off into Berkeley Square.

When I got to bed I slept heavily for a time and then woke absolutely certain that I was lying in the coal cellar and that opposite me in the dark Lynn sat with the dust over her decaying face. I reached for the light and couldn't find it, and that proved I was in the cellar. I started up, climbing out of bed, and heard that terrible dead rattle of the coals. I knocked over the bedside lamp, the shade fell to the floor, and presently I found the switch and pressed it so that the bright light came on with the lamp lying on its side. My dazzled eyes couldn't see into the far corner of the room and I got to the floor clutching the lamp and staring. It took two or three minutes to become sure that in the corner there was only a round white cushion on the arm of a chair.

Then I got back sweating and lay exhausted against the wooden head of the bed.

As I lay there I remembered I'd not switched off the light in the cellar when I hauled the dog out. The light must still be silently burning there, and would stay on all through the night and all through to-morrow unless I went back and saw to it. It wasn't right to leave her in the light. She should be in the dark. There was a decency about the darkness that all humanity needed when it came to its last humiliation. So she had come too young, and was the more horrible because of it.

There grew in me a need to get up at once and take my car out and drive down to Hockbridge so that I could alter all that. It took all my common sense to stay where I was, to be reasonable and logical about it, knowing that she would not know and could not care.

But I didn't go to sleep again.

17

Ray French had a corduroy jacket thrown carelessly across his shoulders, over a silk monogrammed shirt knotted at the throat with a spotted maroon scarf. He raised his eyebrows in an amused sort of way and looked blandly welcoming.

'Come in, old boy. You're an early visitor. We're just finishing breakfast.'

I said: 'Sorry, but I wanted to catch you before you went out.'

'Yes, of course.' He looked at me pretty oddly for a

second, then led the way up the stairs and into a tiny dining-room, from which through double doors you could see into his music-room, a big gaudily-curtained place with a black Steinway piano.

It occurred to me that I hadn't been to his flat before. Like him it was rather a mixture of the orthodox and the flamboyant. There was a second breakfast-cup on the table and a lipstick-stained cigarette-end in its saucer.

He waved a finger towards a chair. 'The coffee won't be nauseating yet. And the cigarettes are on the side-table.'

'Thanks, I've finished. About that postcard you had from Lynn. Do you still have it?'

He frowned with one eyebrow at the cigarette he was lighting. When the thing was going and he had flipped the lighter out with his thumb he said: 'Pressed in lavender. Has it some special significance?'

'It could have.'

'Well, I must say it escapes me; it was only about records.'

He went into the larger room and then disappeared through another door. A large black Persian cat came in by the same door and stretched itself and rubbed a lazy head against the leg of the piano. Then it came slowly into the dining-room and sat on its tail and looked at me with amber eyes. They were like Ray's. On the wall above the cat was a lithograph of Hyde Park in 1820, and beside that a Florentine mirror, in which I was suddenly startled to see black hair move.

I jerked round in my seat and found that Margot du Caine, Ray's fiancée, had come into the room. I got up.

'Good morning! I didn't hear you.'

'Good morning.' She smiled self-consciously, her rather blind-looking eyes going past me in search of Ray.

'We met at Glyndebourne,' I said. 'I don't know if you remember——'

'Yes, of course.' But she didn't.

Second viewing confirmed the first; she looked inexperienced, rather inelegant, trying to hide her unsureness. But she wasn't unattractive in a rather negative way.

'I came for my cigarettes. Oh, yes, here they are.' She picked them up from the chair facing the empty cup. 'Thanks, no,' as I offered my case. 'I won't smoke now.'

We stood about for a few seconds. She put her hands down and straightened her skirt over the hips.

'My name is Granville.' I said. 'Mike Granville.'

She went on looking steadily at nothing, but her fingers had stiffened. Just then Ray came back with the card. He raised his cigarette-end to Margot. ' 'Lo, darling. You two know each other, don't you?'

'Yes,' I said, taking the card, 'thank you.'

'Margot got here just before you, so we decided to work up the breakfast-table atmosphere. Got to get into training for next week.'

The postcard was typewritten, the message very much what he had said over the telephone, including the last phrase, 'Am staying a few days with Hazel at the above address.' The signature was in ink and was the single word 'Lynn.' The postmark was N.W.8.

'Does she often send you typewritten letters?'

'She hasn't often written to me. But, no, I don't remember another typewritten. Why?'

I glanced at the girl and hesitated. Ray's laugh bubbled over. 'I haven't any secrets from Margot.'

'All the same, I think if you don't mind . . .'

Margot turned her stare on Ray. 'Do you want me to go, darling? You know nothing you can say——'

'Nothing I can say. But evidently Mike wants to say and doesn't like.'

'In that case I'll go.' She bent suddenly and picked up the cat. Her mass of dark glossy hair made the cat's coat look lifeless. We watched her move through into the big room, and Ray shut the double doors.

'When is the wedding?' I said.

'Sunday at crack of three. We're spending Sunday night in London and catching the *Otrantes* at Southampton on Monday afternoon. What's the matter, Mike? You look as if you're carrying more than your pay-load.'

'Lynn and I have separated for good.'

He whistled. 'You as much as said that over the phone, but I hoped . . .'

'Ray,' I said, 'you knew Lynn had a flat of her own in Grosvenor Court Mews, didn't you?'

He looked at me and then sat sideways in a chair, put a leg over one of the arms and hitched his jacket round him. 'Whispers, I must confess, have reached my ears.'

'You've been there, of course?'

He examined one of his finger-nails. 'Well, well, how you cover ground!'

'Have you been often?'

He took out a nail file and rubbed off a corner that was worrying him. 'What is this, old boy? Any Questions? It's a trifle early in the morning.'

'It's late in the day for learning the things I am learning.'

'What am I supposed to say?'

'You're not compelled to say anything; but Lynn didn't have that flat for four months just for ornament.'

'Has she had it four months? Good lord!'

'When did you first go there?'

'As a point of no interest whatever, how did you know I'd been?'

'I thought it unlikely that another of my friends smoked these cheroots.'

I put the piece of the cigar band on the table near him.

He stared at it. A muscle in his cheek moved. 'In the blossoms of my sin, eh?'

'What is there between you and Lynn?'

'Would you be surprised if I told you absolutely nothing at all?'

'Very—now.'

'It's the truth—now.'

'Then what *was* there between you?'

'Why don't you ask Lynn?'

'Because I can't find her.'

'But *really*, Mike, but really . . . Put yourself in my place. . . . She'll turn up, and you can ask her then.'

'Lynn was your mistress?' I said.

'Look, old boy——'

'When did it begin?'

He picked up the piece of cigar band and sniffed it. 'I'm not sure that this is mine, you know. Where did you find it?'

'When did it begin?'

He rolled the paper into a ball, flicked it away with finger and thumb. There was a long silence.

'About—four months ago,' he said at last.

'And how long did it go on?'

'Desultorily until the beginning of June.'

'Why did it end?'

He turned and looked at me in a queer way, a bit embarrassed but challenging. 'Lynn just told me one day that she'd had enough. . . . In a sense I was relieved.'

'Why?'

'I'm not un-fond of women, Mike, but carrying on with the wife of a friend isn't my strongest line. And then I had met Margot.'

'Did you quarrel with Lynn?'

'Oh, lord, no! We parted dear friends, still write and phone each other, as you see.'

'Did she give any reason for finishing this—this affair with you?'

'Don't you think you'd better ask her?'

'I'm asking you.'

Ray swung his leg off the chair and put his arms into his jacket. 'This *is* a fact-finding commission, isn't it? Yes, if you want to know, she did give me a reason. She said she'd found someone else.'

'Did she mention a name?'

'Naturally not.'

'Did she say where she'd met him, or anything of that sort?'

'No. . . . She gave me the impression that she'd known him some time, but that suddenly the lid had blown off, as it were.'

131

I thought it all out. 'Were you the first? At Grosvenor Court Mews, I mean?'

Again he glanced me up and down. 'No. In fact there may have been others at the same time. I don't know how often she came to Town.'

'Twice a week.'

He didn't speak but fumbled for another cigarette.

I said: 'When did you last see Lynn?'

'At Glyndebourne when we all met. Eighth of July, wasn't it? But I rang her after that at Hockbridge. Four or five days after.'

'When was it she told you she was leaving me?'

'What? She didn't.'

'You said——'

'Oh, you mean over the phone the last time we spoke. I didn't take it at all that she was leaving you. I simply offered to toil down with the records on the Saturday and she said she'd be away.'

I got up and walked to the window and put out my own cigarette. The storms of yesterday had cleared but the summer spell was over. The sky was grey and low.

He said: 'Look, old boy, I don't want to *blackguard* Lynn; but in fairness to your feelings about me . . . How would you go on if a woman made a dead set at you—and one as damned attractive as Lynn? I'm no angel and have never pretended to be, but I don't go round clocking in for other men unless there's a very big welcome put out. How much do you understand Lynn, Mike?'

'Don't get too big-hearted towards yourself.'

'Well, when you find her, ask her if what I say isn't true. Ask her if I was the first or even the fifth or even——'

'Shut up,' I said.

He shrugged and fastened one of the big leather buttons on his jacket. 'At least I'm glad to feel I'm not the reason she left you.'

'It must be very gratifying.'

'Well, so it is. I've always liked you, Mike, and the fact that you now hate my guts doesn't alter it. So though I fully

132

admit the injury I've done you, I'm relieved it's not as great as it might have been.'

I said: 'You'd talk yourself out of Judgment Day.' And went to the door.

'Wait.' He had flushed. 'One thing. Your marriage is all to Hell, and you blame me and you blame other men and you blame Lynn. Has it ever occurred to you to blame yourself?'

'Quite often.'

'Well, don't.'

I stood watching him.

He said: 'If you want the truth I'll tell you. Lynn's charming and decorative and likeable. But she's a nympho of the first order. No man plays that hand right. If she wants to divorce you, let her. You'll be well out of it.'

18

Some people who haven't actually been in a shooting war get through a good bit of their lives without much contact with death. I had. And when I had come up against it my feeling had been that what's left of a person after death isn't much more important than an old dressing-gown. At first you felt that something must still be around somewhere quite apart from the old worn-out stuff that went into the ground, but common sense dealt with that in the end. The organs of sense that make up one's personality *must* die with the body, so what *can* be left?

The discovery of yesterday seemed to have knocked most of my earlier notions over the ropes. I don't know why, unless it was that this person who had changed into a coppery green horror had been so much a part of my own grown-up life. The feelings it got in me came up from something older than reason. It was as if I'd recognised not only Lynn but some knowledge beyond what I ordinarily knew. It had only been there for a second, but unless I shut my mind down altogether I couldn't funk that it had been there.

Not that there was anything very positive. It was more like a denial of denials. It wasn't that I knew the answers—only that I knew now I didn't know them.

You could say of course that the terrific shock, the fear, the horror, had knocked my intelligence off its perch; but the cause and the effect were not to be confused.

As I got near the works I knew that the one thing I wanted more than anything else in the world just now was to see Stella. She was like an answer, a reassurance. Yes, there was death and corruption but also there was light and life; and perhaps somehow, some way, that beauty and freshness and charm which made up the inexplicable self of a woman and which were so much greater than the sum of their parts—having once been and become greater than themselves could maintain themselves outside time and place and reason.

Outside reason? Yes. Lynn, dead, somehow stipulated it. But it was for Stella, living, that I craved it. For the moment I was willing not to be a reasonable man.

Miss Allen said: 'Good morning, Mr. Granville. We were hoping you were coming this morning. Several things have cropped up rather urgently. Has Mr. Read seen you?'

I looked at the electric clock with its silly lame-man's minute-hand. As I looked it gave one of its clicks and limped to a quarter to twelve.

'No, not yet.'

'Mr. Thurston rang you yesterday afternoon and twice this morning. He said would you ring him as soon as you got in.'

'Right. Give me a minute or two to get sorted out.'

There was a tap and Read came in. 'Morning, Mr. Granville. Everything all right?'

'Yes. Why not?'

'Were you fit yesterday? I mean not turning up at all. . . .'

'I was fit. All right, Miss Allen, I'll call you.'

134

As the girl went out Read said: 'We had merry hell yesterday. But you see the men are still here.'

'What men?'

'The electricians. Surely you knew about it?'

'Oh? . . . Oh, yes. They haven't struck, then?'

'No, I got a wedge in between Gill and Piper. After all it's none of Piper's bloody business and Gill's our shop steward. To my surprise, Burgin helped.'

'Burgin?'

'Yes, he turned against his pal and took the reasonable side. It's due to him that the ballot's been put off till to-morrow or Monday. I'll hand it to him that he took what you told him the right way.'

I tried to think what I'd told him. It seemed a month ago. 'If this ever gets as far as an official union matter . . .'

Read shrugged. 'We either take McGowrie back or there won't be an electrician within miles. That's certain. You know the E.T.U.'

When he had gone I realised I ought to have had it out with him how the truth about McGowrie's dismissal had leaked out. But somehow I didn't think Read was at fault. I had a hunch that perhaps Dawson had been the one to talk too much. Perhaps Frank was at the bottom of more than I realised.

I pressed the inter-com thing and told Miss Allen I wanted to see Mrs. Curtis.

'She's not here to-day, sir. She phoned to say she couldn't get in.'

'Oh.'

'She asked to speak to you. She rang about eleven.'

'Oh, thanks.' So the decision was made for me. 'Will you tell Mr. Dawson I want to see him.'

'Mr. Dawson's gone down to Wales. He said he'd told you about it last night.'

'Oh . . . yes . . . I'd forgotten. When did he leave?'

'I'm not sure, Mr. Granville. Er—shall I get Harwell for you?'

'Yes, please.'

I drew prison bars on my blotting pad until the call came through.

Thurston said: 'We've fixed a full meeting for three o'clock to-morrow afternoon.'

'Where? At Harwell?'

'No, at Llanveryan. There's a man called Holborn going to be there, from Chalk River. He's on a visit to England, and he's one of the men who's been building scintillometers for aerial prospecting in Canada. Bennett thought it would be a good idea to have him in for his expert advice and to give a deciding opinion on Steel's criticisms.'

'I don't like the sound of that,' I said.

'Nor I. Because I think it will be a deciding opinion on the instrument as a whole. But I hear Holborn's a very sensible bloke. I don't think he'd take any narrow view.'

'Why is everybody going down to Llanveryan?'

'That's what I rang you about. Holborn wants to test our equipment as thoroughly as he can before he gives a considered opinion of it. So we've fixed a trial for eleven to-morrow. You can be there by then?'

'Yes,' I said, and knew I couldn't. I knew I couldn't be there at all.

'We can't go up with him, of course, but it's very important we should both be on the spot. We ought to try to talk to him before the others come along.'

When he'd rung off I sat a while longer making the prison more realistic. I couldn't go down to-morrow because this afternoon I had to go to Greencroft to discover the body of my wife. I doubted if even Harwell had the pull to get me released on bail. Of course men from Chalk River, experts in this fairly rare corner of electronic development, didn't come over here for holidays—at least they didn't appear suddenly and accidentally at just the right moment. It was perfectly clear that Thurston was right and that Holborn had been sent for the specific purpose of deciding how far Steel's criticisms were valid. To-morrow I might have to fight for all the things I considered worth while in our design. I might

136

have *had* to fight for them. Now I should not be there. But anyway nothing mattered any more.

I had some sort of a late lunch with all these things milling in my head. Afterwards I drove down to Greencroft.

It was no good pretending I'd been into the cellar; there had to be anthracite dust on my shoes and on my hands. I wondered if twenty-four hours would have changed her. The disturbance of yesterday . . . As well after all that I hadn't seen Stella, while this other hand was on me.

I thought of calling in for Kent, but couldn't tolerate the idea of his being allowed down again. Anyway it was unnecessary. I hadn't to provide a reason for going into the cellar of my own house.

I stopped the car where the mouth of the drive broadened out before the house. The house looked chill and deserted. There was no thunder to-day, but a grey wind blew across the garden and rustled the leaves of the laurels. The antirrhinums, in the bed where the tulips had been, were nearly over; the faded brown flower stalks were sticky with decay. I cut off the engine and slid my fingers round the steering wheel; it was warm and clammy from the grip of my hands. Even the backs of my hands were clammy. I opened the door and got out. My knees were no good. It all had to happen to-day as it should have happened yesterday. At least I wouldn't have to sham feeling queer. It was going to be all I could do to get as far as the cellar. I shut the car door quietly, got out the key of the house, turned it round twice and then began to walk towards the front door. My feet crunched noisily on the gravel, like the sound of someone walking on crisp snow. It was queer because it was as if there was an echo of my own footsteps. It was as if I had four feet or was being followed. The cloven hoof. Like one that on a lonely road. At the door I stopped dead, my hair prickling, and turned. There was no one behind me, but the crunching footsteps were going on. . . .

They were coming towards me round the corner of the house. The day had never been more chill than it was at that moment. Then a woman came round the corner. It was Stella.

19

She said: 'What luck! I came hoping to find you——'

'Stella, what the *hell* are you doing here?'

She stopped, her eyes moving quickly over my face. 'What's the matter?'

I tried to put a brake on. 'Nothing. . . . You startled me. Phew, it was a fright!'

'*Sorry.* Did you think it was Lynn back?'

'No. . . . I didn't think it was Lynn back. . . . How on earth did you get here?'

'By train. It isn't difficult. This end there's a walk.'

'But what made you come? Is John——?'

'No, I was worried about you.'

'Why?'

'Well, you weren't at the works yesterday and you promised to call in and see us in the evening.'

I wanted to sit down somewhere. 'But did you know I would be here?'

'No, I came over on the off chance.'

I put my hand out and took her fingers. 'You don't know how much I've longed to see you these last two days. You never will know.' She looked at me almost in surprise. 'Stella, it's the sober truth. I'm making nothing up. Every hour. . . .'

She seemed very touched. 'Mike, dear——'

'And I'm not forgetting anything. But you shouldn't have come. It's better at present that we aren't seen together, so I won't ask you in——'

'Oh, I've been in,' she said.

I felt as if all the blood had run into my feet. 'You've—been in?'

'Did you mind? You told me about the key under the geranium for Lynn. I found it there. It was stuffy in the

138

house so I'd just opened the french windows when I heard your car.'

I tried to swallow and gave it up and let her hand fall. 'Have you been here long?'

'No. I waited five minutes and then thought of going home. But the next train is four-thirty.'

'I'll take you back,' I said. 'We can talk in the car.'

Little lines gathered about her eyes as she looked at me. 'What's happened, Mike? Why didn't you come last evening?'

'I'll tell you in the car.'

'I suppose it's better not to be seen here.'

'Much better. I———'

'We ought to lock the french windows before we leave, oughtn't we? Sorry I trespassed.'

'You go and sit in the car. I'll lock up and join you.'

She hesitated. 'All right.'

I watched her walk to the car. She was wearing a light tan coat, and although there was no sun the wind seemed to shine in her hair. I went in.

I got across the hall without looking towards the kitchen. It was more than stuffy. I went into the drawing-room and shut the windows. Nothing had altered from yesterday. Nothing had breathed or stirred or *lived* in the room. I came out and through the hall and shut the front door after me.

When I got to the car Stella was lighting a cigarette. She didn't look at me when I got in. She put out her lighter and slipped it into her bag.

'I don't know why I can't stop smoking,' she said. 'Until this week my average was about three a day.'

'What happened to the key?'

'Here.'

'Thanks.'

'Perhaps we should put it back just in case.'

'Perhaps.'

My hand was on the wheel, and she put hers over it. I bent and kissed her fingers and then leaned my face against them.

139

'Darling, what is it?'

'Just keep on saying that,' I said.

'I wish I could. I wouldn't want anything better.'

'Stella . . .'

'I know. It doesn't sound like self-denial week. Sorry. . . .'

'Don't ever be sorry for what you've just said.'

'It—isn't any good being, now that it's out. But I didn't come here to say it.'

'I know.' I raised my head. 'What was that?'

'Nothing as far as I know. What did you think?'

'Let's go.'

I told her about finding the key and going to Lynn's flat. I told her all the rest from there. I realised that for the first time I was lying—by omission—to her, just as she was lying by omission to her husband. We talked, but all the time I was on edge to get away from the house. At last I switched on the ignition and started the engine. We made a half-circle and back and moved away slowly. Whatever else, the discovery was off for this afternoon——

As we turned the corner of the drive to the road, I braked hard. A car was stopped a couple of yards inside the drive and a man was standing with his hand on the door, either just getting in or just getting out. When my tyres slithered he left his own car and came towards us. He was a man of about forty in a bowler hat and a dark suit with speckled trousers and highly polished black shoes. There was a circular mark on his cheek like a vaccination mark, and he had a tight mouth with a full bottom lip.

He took off his hat when he saw Stella. To me he said: 'I beg your pardon, this is Greencroft, isn't it?'

I said it was, and wondered if he was going to push another petition into my hand.

'And are you Mr. Granville?'

'Yes.'

'Oh, my name is Baker. Detective-Sergeant Baker. I wonder if you could spare me a few minutes of your time?'

'I can hardly refuse it.'

He smiled without looking amused and put his hands

140

behind his back. 'That has been known. Er—you were coming away from the house?'

'Yes. This is my technical assistant, Mrs. Curtis.'

He inclined his head. 'I won't keep you long, Mr. Granville; but we're making a few inquiries, and I thought——'

'Inquiries about what?'

He looked surprised, as if he thought he'd told me or as if he thought I ought to know. 'About your wife, Mr. Granville.'

I noticed he was wearing a stiff white collar with a blue striped shirt, and his black tie was pulled into a tiny knot. He had a cultured voice that didn't sound as if it had been with him all his life. Even his smile was tough.

I said: 'What was it you wanted to know?'

Baker glanced at Stella. 'Would it be convenient if we went back to the house?'

'. . . Unfortunately we can't,' I said. 'I'm living in Letherton and forgot the key. Would you like to drive along there with me? It's only twenty minutes.'

'Well, I don't think that will be necessary. Perhaps a few minutes' conversation . . .'

'I'll walk on,' Stella said. 'Catch me up, Mr. Granville, will you?'

'No, there's no need to do that,' I protested, but she opened the door and slid out. Our eyes met for a second through the glass as she shut the door.

'I'll take the road for the village,' she said. 'Don't miss me, will you?' She smiled at Sergeant Baker, and he raised his hat again.

We watched her for a moment. 'Shall I get out of the car, or will you get in?'

'I don't think either's really necessary,' he said. 'I was really quite lucky to catch you, then?'

'Has my wife sent you?'

'No, not exactly.' He ran a hand along the panel of the door.

'I was served with a petition for divorce this week. It rather jaundices one's attitude towards strange officials.'

141

'Your wife is divorcing you, Mr. Granville?'

'That's her idea.'

His glance strayed past me and down the road, as if to look at Stella again. 'No, I came really to inquire if you knew where your wife was at the moment.'

'I wish I did.'

'Yes. Yes, so do we.'

'Don't tell me the police want her for something.'

He put out his bottom lip. 'We're making a few inquiries at the instigation of her bank. When did you last see her, Mr. Granville?'

'Three weeks ago yesterday morning. When I got home in the evening she wasn't there, and the following morning I had a letter from her telling me she was leaving me.'

'Do you still have the letter?'

'Yes.'

'I'd rather like to see it sometime.'

'Is it of special interest?'

'Well, it could be. You see, her bank have had two communications from her since then, and they are not satisfied about her signature.'

I looked at him and he looked back at me.

'What do they suggest?'

'I think they prefer to leave it to others to suggest. They are merely—dissatisfied.'

I got out of the car and took out my pocket-book. 'I've carried her letter ever since. I think it's here.'

'You haven't heard from her since?'

'No.' I gave him the letter.

He read it. 'Are you satisfied that this is your wife's handwriting?'

'Yes.'

'Do you know if she ever signed herself Lynn Granville in her business affairs?'

'I don't think so in her formal dealings. She used her full name Lindsey.'

'Yes, that's what the bank said. Er—were you surprised when she left you, Mr. Granville?'

142

'Very.'

'You didn't expect her to petition for a divorce?'

'Certainly I didn't.'

'What were the grounds?'

I put the letter away. 'I have a feeling that you know all this already.'

He smiled slightly and glanced down and moved the signet ring round on the little finger of his right hand. 'Why should I?'

'If the bank have reported that someone has been forging my wife's signature, it's natural to begin general inquiries.'

'These *are* the general inquiries, Mr. Granville.'

'But not the beginning of them.'

'Not quite the beginning of them.'

A wasp came between us for a moment, settled on the bonnet of the car and moved with angular venomous legs across the slippery surface. Baker waved it away.

'Were you aware that your wife had a flat in London?'

'Not before she left me. I've discovered it since.'

'And have you been there?'

'Yes, two or three times, but there was no one in.'

'There was someone in last night. The lady below phoned for the police, but the man escaped through a window.'

'Man? It wasn't Lynn, then?'

'Apparently there was a struggle. Can you give me any leads as to where you think your wife might be?'

I took out my cigarette-case and offered him a cigarette. He smiled and shook his head and I put my case away.

'I don't know what you know of my movements in the last four or five days, Sergeant Baker. But if you check them you'll find that since I had this divorce petition I've thrown over my work and everything else in trying to find her.'

'Did you make no effort to find her before that? I should have thought the incentive would have been greater then.'

'The bank will tell you I did.'

'Only the bank?'

'I rang her mother and every friend of hers I could trace.'

143

'Have you felt worried about what might have happened to her?'

'No. I take it she's lying low somewhere for her own purposes.'

'Which are?'

I said: 'I don't quite follow you. Do you think something has happened to her?'

'Not necessarily at all. In any case the bank may be quite mistaken in their doubt as to her signature. Certainly the letters were typed on the machine which is in her flat.'

'I see you've already been pretty thorough.'

'We do our best. Tell me, Mr. Granville, is the lady who was with you the—er—woman named, as they call it, in the divorce petition?'

'I'm sure you know that she is.'

'She is married, I understand?'

'Yes, and happily.'

'To an invalid husband?'

'Does that surprise you?'

'Frankly, in this work after a while one loses one's capacity for surprise. But on the law of averages I'd say that an attractive young woman, married to a sick and older man——'

'I should have thought you would have learned to distrust the law of averages as well.'

He smiled, this time with his eyes too. 'That seems a very fair come-back. Have you gone through your wife's papers since she left?'

'I looked through some of them yesterday.'

'No help?'

'No help at all.'

He took his hand off the headlamp of the car. 'Well, thank you, Mr. Granville. We'll carry on with our inquiries. We don't, of course, for the moment propose to list Mrs. Granville among the "missing persons". There may be some very simple explanation of the whole thing. Where can I find you if I want you again?'

'Care of the Old Bull, Letherton. And you?'

'I think I'll have to back before you can get past.' He stared with suspicious brown eyes at his own car, as if he thought it guilty of loitering with intent. 'Me? Oh, you can phone me direct in London or practically care of any police station.'

I left him sitting in his car watching me drive away.

I said to Stella: 'I lied to that fellow about the key for several reasons. One was that I didn't want him to think we'd spent the whole afternoon alone in the house together.'

'So he thinks Lynn has disappeared?'

'He's only guessing.'

'But—the signatures that the bank are complaining of—were they on cheques?'

'No, on letters, I think.'

We drove on.

I said: 'Stella . . .'

'Yes?'

'Oh, nothing.'

'What were you going to say?'

'It doesn't matter. Will you invite me to supper to-night?'

'Of course. Come in now. There'll only be an hour to wait.'

'Will John be well enough to see me?'

'Oh, yes. He's in bed, but . . .'

'Do you want me to say I picked you up in the town?'

She was silent. 'More than anything I hate lying to him.'

'On this I don't think we need or should.'

We had come to the outskirts of Letherton. I wondered what Baker was doing now I'd left him. Was he driving back to London, or was he still at Greencroft, walking round the house and peering in at the windows? I hoped I had locked the french windows both top and bottom.

Coming to a sudden decision, I said: 'I want very much to have a talk with John.'

She looked at me. 'What about?'

'About this policeman's visit.'

20

John Curtis pushed himself farther up the pillows, and then impatiently flattened the sheet. You could still see the power in his hands. For two or three minutes he hadn't spoken—not since I stopped. Downstairs I could hear Stella as she moved about getting supper.

Though he was a pretty straightforward man, I couldn't tell what he was thinking. You wouldn't know until he wanted you to know.

Without looking at me he said: 'Why do you tell *me* this?'

'I'm out of my depth. I thought if anyone could advise me on the motions of self-preservation it would be you.'

'Is self-preservation all you want?'

'Not all.'

His face was tight-drawn, the brilliant brown eyes concentrated as if in a bright light. 'You realise you've taken a vital step in telling me all this?'

'Yes.'

'And a risk?'

'The risk of being disbelieved. I know.'

'Oh, I believe you.'

'That's a risk you take.'

He shook his head. 'You're not a murderer. You've too much imagination. And tolerance. Though I think you might have put them both to better uses.'

'. . . Unfortunately the police deal only in proof.'

'No, the risk you've taken in telling me this is that you've, so to speak, passed the baby on to me. Whether you do as I advise or not, I have to tell the police or get in a tricky position myself.'

I went to the window and sat in the window-seat. 'And what do you advise?'

'Tell me first about yourself and your wife. Tell me about

146

things on the periphery of the story. I want to see more of the picture.'

I tried to tell him about all the people distantly or closely involved, Simon Heppelwhite and Ray French and Frank Dawson and our life together before she disappeared. 'The trouble is,' I said, 'that the whole equation isn't laid on. Bits of it are probably floating around Lynn's London flat and the men who visited her there.'

Footsteps were coming upstairs. John waited but they went past. He said: 'An equation can have unknown quantities. The real difficulty lies in setting the thing up.'

'It's in trying to set it up—or break it down—that I've landed myself in a worse mess than before.'

'This man Simon Heppelwhite. He's your best friend and hers. If he's not involved he could have a clearer view of your marriage than anyone. Have you seen him recently?'

'Not since this thing blew its top off.'

'He would be worth seeing. There must be a reason why he appeared to turn against Lynn, as you say he did. And why has your wife been meeting this man from your works, Dawson? I——'

'The answer looks fairly obvious to me.'

He tried to take a deep breath and failed. 'This man French tells you that your wife was a nymphomaniac. What do you say? You should know.'

I said bitterly: 'Perhaps I don't.'

'But what would you have said?'

'I should have called her highly sexed. I'd no reason to suppose more.'

'Perhaps a nymphomaniac doesn't need to appear more than that to any one man. Why should she? Especially to her husband, whom it's more necessary to deceive than anyone else. And yet I wonder . . .'

Silence fell between us.

He said: 'How exactly did the body look? Can you describe it in more detail?'

I described it in more detail. He said: 'Yes . . . Of course we're supposing that the police will be able to fix the date of

147

her death accurately. That may not be. When a body is left exposed to the air, an estimate's much easier because the calliphora which normally breed on the body go through definite life cycles, and you can calculate accurately by their evolution. But anthracite, I should think—— This upsets you?'

'Go on.'

'Anthracite would have some of the semi-preservative properties of ordinary soil. Was she completely covered?'

'I think she must have been. The dog . . . She isn't now.'

'She isn't now. So from now on things will move more quickly. Well, if she has been completely covered I doubt if the pathologists will be able to specify the date of her death to within four or five days. . . . But are you sure?'

'I think she died the night she disappeared.'

'Then who came back the following night and what did they come for?'

'I think the person who killed her had left something behind and wanted to get it. . . . The scent came from the bottle he'd upset. And I think the ear-ring had been lying there since the night before.'

'But your wife must have intended to divorce you. She must have sworn the affidavit when she was still alive.'

'Yes, and I think she must have meant to leave me that night. The letter she wrote to me was so typical, and her handwriting is particularly hard to copy.'

'But you believe she didn't pack her own bag?'

'I'm certain she didn't complete it anyway. She wouldn't under *any* circumstances pack my toothpaste. She always hated the flavour. She'd be as likely to pack my shoes by mistake.'

'The point I think we have to ask ourselves, since it's the first question the police will ask themselves, is who stands in any way to benefit from your wife's death. What was the motive: profit, concealment, reputation, sex, anger, jealousy? And how was the murder done?'

'Her—present condition shouldn't prevent them from discovering that.'

'No. . . .'

'And what do you advise me to do?' I said again.

Outside on the weedy lawn a long black cat was stalking a thrush. In the branch of a distorted elm another thrush was making an excited twittering sound.

'Go and see a good criminal lawyer first thing in the morning. It's the only way, Mike. Don't go within a mile of your house again. Go and see him and tell him everything and do whatever he advises.'

'Which will be to see the police at once.'

'Yes, but in his presence. You'll be in a far stronger position after you've consulted him.'

'Another lawyer . . .'

'As a matter of fact I think I know the man who would do—I was at school with him—Digby Hamilton. At the moment he's right at the top.'

The black cat had got very near the bird now. His hind quarters quivered with the intent to kill. The thrush had taken no heed of his friend's warning. Then almost as the cat launched himself, the thrush saw the danger and flung open his wings. A quick flutter put him just out of reach of the flying claws, and then he gathered height and soared into the tree.

'If I don't take your advice?'

'That's to be decided.'

'Doing what you say wouldn't keep Stella out of the picture.'

'Perhaps nothing will.'

'Yes, but if I was arrested and charged they might think she had some knowledge of it—if we're supposed to be lovers. She might be dragged in as an accessory after the fact.'

'The danger's there, but it will be there now whatever you do. Actually, even if you were the murderer and they convicted you, they couldn't find enough evidence to move against her.'

'Only to poison the rest of her life with ugly rumours.'

'The surest way of avoiding that is to clear yourself, and

the surest way of clearing yourself is to see someone like Digby Hamilton.'

I got up and walked across the room. Now that it came to the point I shied away from the sort of thing I'd been going to do three hours earlier. Detective-Sergeant Baker's arrival on the scene had made everything infinitely more difficult.

'Oh, of course, I know you're right; it's the logical, sensible thing to do. But telling you about it—even though you've believed me—has made me realise what a lame-duck story it really sounds. I wish I could make one more positive step of some sort before giving away my freedom of action. For instance, I feel I ought to follow up this note from Frank Dawson.'

'He's in Wales at present?'

'Yes, I had promised to go down myself to-morrow. This survey job is in its last stages.'

'The police will find out all that Dawson has to tell.'

'Where does Hamilton live?' I asked, partly to gain time.

'We should find him at his flat in the Temple. He might even see you to-night. I did him a favour a couple of years ago and I don't think he'd refuse.'

I picked up the book he had put down when I came in, stared at it, trying to decide. 'Do you read Greek for pleasure?'

'I've never had time since I left school. And I was pretty bad at it there.'

'So you're making up time now.'

'Something like that.'

I shook my head. 'I'm sorry but it doesn't make sense.'

'To improve my Greek? Why, because I'm dying? We all are. Mine is only an accelerated rate.'

'I hope not too accelerated.'

A thrush was still chattering in the garden.

'There are days when I feel much better,' he said. 'Have you decided, Mike?'

'Give me until after supper.'

Footsteps again, and Stella put her head in. 'Sorry to be

150

an age. Things are nearly done. If Mike will give me a hand upstairs with them. . . .'

'No,' said John. 'Have it downstairs. I'd rather come down.'

'But only a few hours ago the doctor said——'

'I'll take the risk. I have a phone call to make this evening.'

While she was fixing things below I helped him to get up, to put on an old fisherman's jersey, a pair of trousers and a coat. He was a queer sight, taller than I was, athletic of build but his vigour in ruins. He was more like someone in the prime of life, injured and having lost blood in a car crash.

When he was dressed he sat on the bed and got his breath back before having a shot at the stairs.

He said rather carefully: 'You know in all this there's one symbol that puzzles me more than it should, because it's the one I'm most familiar with. It's the letter S—which shouldn't be an unknown quantity to me at all.'

I reached for his slippers under the bed, found one, and then took more time than I needed to find the other.

Hoping my voice sounded right, I said: 'We've agreed she's not really in it at all.'

'Oh, she is in one sense, whether we like it or not.'

'Are these slippers the right way round?—there doesn't seem any difference.'

'There isn't. . . . Are you in love with Stella, Mike?'

I would have given a year then to have been still in search of the slipper. But I wasn't. He only had to put his foot into it, and there was nothing I could do but straighten up.

I straightened up. I looked at him. He had his finger inside the heel of the slipper, fixing it.

'Yes, John. I think I am.' There wasn't any lie I could tell him at all. Not any.

'Only think you are?'

'No. . . . I'm sure.'

'And does Stella love you?' As he spoke he lifted his own

head, his face a little less colourless from bending, his eyes full of a sort of incredulous inquiry.

'You ought to know she doesn't.'

Slowly he buttoned his coat, the strong fingers fumbling but not only from weakness.

He said: 'One isn't responsible for one's emotions, only for one's actions. . . . Perhaps I should feel gratified that we have an admiration in common——'

'I've only known it for the last four or five days. Believe me, I'd no idea . . .'

'One doesn't necessarily have, until the last minute.'

'I thought I felt the same as ever about Lynn. It must strike you as queer, phoney——'

'Not as much as it might. Because something rather like it happened to me.'

There was a whistle from downstairs. He mastered his own lips and whistled back.

'When I met Stella my first wife had only been dead two months. I'd been married to her for sixteen years, and marriages aren't much better than ours had been. When she died I thought everything was finished for ever. If I hadn't by accident met Stella it might have been. But you would have thought chance would have given me a year or so to grieve decently. When I found myself in love with Stella—and deeply and truly in love: not merely wanting her and finding marriage the only way of getting her—when I found myself in love, the feeling for a long time came up against a sense of outraged decency; it seemed to put in question my own sincerity towards both women and my honesty with myself. . . . Did you feel anything like that?'

'Very much. . . . Only I hadn't reasoned it right out. But in my case there's—an extra difficulty.'

'You mean that Stella isn't free,' he said gently. 'But S becomes part of the equation.'

'I still don't see it. Except that anything I may feel for her—any wish to keep her from getting her feet muddied— may have a bearing on what I do, she still isn't anywhere but on the extreme outside edge of this mess; and that I hope is where she's going to stay.'

He said: 'Consider the significance of a point which travels round the circumference of an ellipse at a uniform rate. . . .' He got up and steadied himself against the bed. 'I wonder if in this problem there is no centripetal force. . . . Shall we go down?'

John Curtis rang his lawyer friend while Stella was upstairs making his bed. For some reason I couldn't explain to myself, I didn't want to be the one to tell Stella about Lynn—I felt I couldn't get the words out which would break that bit of news. It was like confession to a crime, merely to admit what I had to admit, and that as a result she had been in the same house with Lynn that afternoon. If John told her in his own time, at least there would be no risk of my having to see the look in her eyes when she knew.

Digby Hamilton was in Paris, his wife said, but she was expecting him back in the morning. John covered the phone and asked me if he should ring someone else, but I said, no, I'd rather see the man he knew; so it was agreed I should ring him at ten in the morning from the hotel. John said he would ring also, to be sure that Hamilton got the right impression as to the urgency of the thing.

I stayed at the cottage until ten. Stella walked to the gate with me when I left. She said: 'It's been a queer evening, Mike. Everyone—walled up, on their best behaviour, safe subjects only. Have we all got secrets from each other?'

'Yes. . . . Stella, he knows that I love you.'

'*Why?* How?'

'He asked me. When it came to the point I found I couldn't lie to him about it. In fact I think he knew.'

'It wouldn't be hard to guess, would it? You—don't seem able to hide it.'

'I'm *sorry.*'

'What did he say?'

'He asked me if you loved me too.'

She put her fingers on the gate. 'Well?'

153

'I said he ought to know that you didn't. I think he believed what I said. But the ice is thin.'

'Do you know why I really came to Hockbridge this afternoon?'

'No, I——'

'It was to say I didn't think I could go on without telling him.'

After a while I said: 'Don't you sometimes hurt a man more by telling him the truth than by lying to him?'

'But when someone has absolute *trust* in you ...' She moved angrily, defensively. 'If I don't play straight in this it makes a sham of everything I do for him. The faithful loving ministering wife ...'

I thought it out, trying to be absolutely honest with myself, trying not to let other considerations crowd us.

'But it isn't a sham; because it's true. You are the faithful loving ministering wife. If he's *got* to know about us, then I'm willing to face it; but I don't think we should insist on telling him because of some discomfort in ourselves. We're not entitled to make him sleep worse at nights so that we can sleep better. The thing's our burden, not his. If we unload it, we're not nobler, we're squaring our consciences at his expense.'

She said: 'If I cared for him less I should care for myself a lot more.'

We were going to separate then, but I made a slight movement towards her. 'No, Mike,' she whispered. 'Everything will become impossible if you——'

'I *know*,' I said, not able to explain the conflict even to her. 'I wasn't going to ... But a lot of things may happen before we meet again.'

'What sort of things?'

'Ask John to-morrow.'

'What sort of things?'

'Darling, I can't tell you. . . . Let me say good night to you now.'

So I kissed the inside of her hand and left her. Even that respectful gesture made my heart thump and wasn't gone

154

through without feeling that I was blundering over the boundaries of the peculiar thing that had built up between the three of us. But perhaps love and betrayal are always nearer to each other than we realise.

21

When I got back to the Old Bull I went straight to bed but couldn't sleep, dozing a dozen times and starting awake again as if sleep were an enemy. My thoughts were on the edge of a precipice; to let go would be to fall into the pit. But in the end I couldn't last out any longer and I suppose about four I gave in. Then, oddly, there was no nightmare about the expected things: it was about the scintillometer and the trials at Llanveryan. I thought the man Holborn from Canada had come to the conference and was shooting the whole of our work and theories to pieces. The thing about it was that he seemed in the dream to use arguments that a misguided but knowledgeable man might have used in real life if he'd wanted to sink the whole idea. I had to answer him. That was obvious. I had to answer him; and in the madly silly way that dreams have I got to my feet and then couldn't remember any of the figures we'd worked out. I'd begin: 'But in a case of that sort the rate-meter output shows a characteristic pattern. Where u is the effective gamma-ray absorption of air, you can express it as $F(t) = I$ $oe - u$ over . . .' and then I wouldn't be able to remember what it was over and knew in any case that I'd left something out. So it went on. Each time I'd try to justify what we'd done, and each time I was pushed into a corner. When the phone went to tell me it was eight o'clock I was in a sweat and knew that the whole of our work was going to be thrown over for an enormous gadget that he had made and which I was absolutely certain would let them down as soon as they got out in the desert.

Before getting up I lit a cigarette and smoked it slowly, watching the smoke as it drifted across the room. Then I had a bath and breakfasted quietly in the over-timbered drawing-room among the pewter and the willow-pattern. There was a paper on the next table and I saw a heading which said: 'State of Emergency in Southern Sudan. Eighty Killed.' I thought, of course Thurston will keep his end up and can probably hold his own with them all on the theoretical side; but it's on the practical side that he'll be outpointed. But anyway, how important *is* our equipment? Can it do something in these peculiar circumstances that no other equipment can? If I believe it can, then it's important it should be approved, for much larger reasons than petty personal ones, and important it should be used irrespective of what happens to the man who made it, or to his factory. What was it Porter from the Foreign Office had said in his rather florid way—'necessary to England'? At half-past nine I phoned Bouverie 6775.

A woman answered and I gave my name and stated my business.

'Oh, is that Mr. Granville,' she said. 'This is Mrs. Hamilton. Dr. Curtis rang about you last evening, didn't he? I'm very sorry but my husband has been delayed in Paris. He rang me late last night and hopes now to be home on the last plane to-night.'

'Oh,' I said.

'From what Dr. Curtis said, your business is rather urgent, isn't it? I don't know if you have anyone else in mind whom you would like to approach instead.'

'No. No, I haven't.'

'My husband's office would be able to recommend some-one. . . . Or if you can wait that long, ring to-morrow any time after nine.'

'Sunday morning?'

'Oh, yes, that won't matter. I mentioned Dr. Curtis's call to Digby, and he said he would certainly see you as soon as he got home.'

I thought it out. 'Is your husband likely to be detained again?'

'He can't be. There are several things needing attention before Monday.'

'And I shall be adding to them.'

'I don't think he would look on it in that light.'

I considered again. 'Thank you, Mrs. Hamilton, I'll phone you to-morrow.'

I hung up and rubbed my hand along the sore place at the back of my head. Then I rang Stella. I said: 'Stella, don't disturb John. Give him a message, will you? Tell him not to bother ringing Digby Hamilton this morning. Tell him Hamilton isn't home to-day but that I've arranged to meet him to-morrow. And tell him I'm going to spend to-day at Llanveryan.'

All the roads were crowded, it being a summer Saturday morning, but I drove as if there was a posse of police cars on my wheels, and got to Llanveryan about ten past two. There I found no trials had taken place in the morning after all because the plane had broken an oil feed and wouldn't be ready to take off for some hours yet. This at first looked like a stroke of luck.

Holborn was a big sharp-boned fellow of forty-odd with nothing much to say and a cagey expression. When I met him he was talking to Steel, who hailed me as if I were an old golfing friend. But I didn't believe a word of it this time. I had five minutes alone with Thurston but didn't get to speak to Frank Dawson at all because, everyone else having arrived, it was decided to have a preliminary meeting right away.

Thurston led off with a highly technical account of the test trials so far. Porter was there, and I wondered what he made of it. Almost certainly nothing at all. Then after we'd discussed them Bennett asked what were Mr. Holborn's impressions so far as they at present went?

Holborn picked up a pencil in his big bony hands and said that obviously he couldn't as of here and now say much about the practical operation of the equipment. Running the apparatus in the plane on the ground had given him the impression that it was a little more sensitive to cosmic radiation than his own, and it seemed to him a pity that no cosmic cancellation circuit had been incorporated. He made one or two other minor comments but didn't mention what most of us had in mind. Steel said:

'And as to the absence of a radioaltimeter?'

Holborn put the pencil behind his ear. 'You're asking me to talk out of turn, Dr. Steel. But in principle I should say that's quite a disadvantage. It increases the likelihood of error—either error in mistaking worthless activity for a valuable ore body or in overlooking the genuine deposit when you come on it.'

Thurston said: 'The risk of error is always there. Without discussing the merits of this particular instrument, the increase of risk must depend largely on the type of country you're prospecting.'

'Oh, yes, surely. Our machine was designed for rugged country. The flatter the terrain, the less your altitude varies as your plane passes over it in level flight. That stands to reason.'

Bennett said: 'I think we have to take into consideration the circumstances for which this particular instrument is designed. And I think before going any further we should hear from Mr. Thurston his reasons for considering this device and then rejecting it.'

Thurston looked at me and said: 'This is really your territory, Granville.'

I said: 'What sort of a plane were you flying, Mr. Holborn?'

'At first we had an Anson V, and then we put it in a Beechcraft Expeditor.'

'Much bigger planes than the Auster we're using. . . .'

'Oh, yes, twice the size. Our apparatus was altogether bigger.'

'And by how much did the radioaltimeter increase the weight?'

'I suppose by about thirty-five pounds.'

I said: 'That was one of our objections. Another is that

you need elaborate test gear that has to be carted from place to place. And at the end it didn't seem to us that one ever has a reliable signal-to-height relationship. It was better, we reasoned, to have no correction than one that couldn't be trusted.'

'Also,' said Thurston, 'you need a highly technical personnel on the spot, first for constant checking and second to interpret the results.'

'Don't you always need a technical personnel?' Holborn discovered a second pencil and drew gentle figure eights on the table-top with it. 'But don't get me wrong. I think there's an area of misunderstanding in our conversation. Are you supposing that we used an altimeter with an automatic electronic compensator?' He looked round the table inquiringly.

'That was my impression,' said Bennett.

'Well, it's wrong, sir. It's used on some of the American machines, but we considered it and discarded it for some of the reasons Mr. Granville has put forward. We simply have a radioaltimeter and an aerial camera, both continuously running, and each can then be compared with the record of the counting rate-meter and any significant signals checked against variations in height and terrain.'

No one spoke for a bit. Steel blew his nose noisily.

Flight Lieutenant Rhodes said: 'But the additional weight will still remain?'

'Yes, the additional weight I told you still remains.'

Rhodes said to Porter: 'This unrest in the Sudan, sir. Is it near our piece of country?'

Porter looked over the top of his spectacles. 'The territory to be prospected was at one time part of Equatoria, where the chief rioting is taking place, and the tribes are still emotionally linked.'

Rhodes said: 'I can only just get her completely airborne now. If I carry another two and half stone of equipment we'll *have* to reduce the fuel carried.'

'Or use a bigger plane,' said Steel.

We talked for a while and then Bennett said: 'I don't

think we can really go any further until Mr. Holborn has had a chance to test the instrument in flight. Do you know when the plane will be ready?'

'About five, I hope,' said Rhodes.

We broke up then. At five I went out to the plane, but the mechanics said it would be another hour yet. On the way back I saw Dawson crossing the tarmac with his limping walk. I fell into step beside him.

'Walk with me as far as the end of the runway,' I said. 'There's something I want to ask you.'

'What's the matter, has Read joined the Communist Party?'

'Frank, when was the last time you saw Lynn?'

He cocked his head, bright-eyed, sardonic, narrow-lipped. 'Lynn? I don't remember. Ages. Why?'

'We've broken up. Did you know?'

Rather surprisingly he flushed. 'When?'

'A few weeks ago. Can you remember when you last saw her?'

'What's gone wrong between you?'

'When did you last see her?'

'. . . Oh, it would be February, I suppose; that time she came down to the works just after we'd moved. I don't get the chance now of dropping round for a drink the way I did in London. I miss that, you know.'

'I had to go through some of her things on Thursday night and found this.' I took out the scribbled message and handed it to him. I knew it already by heart, and watched him frowning at it as if the writing were too small for him to read. We had stopped, and the afternoon sun coming suddenly through the clouds fell on us like a klieg light.

He said: 'This was written ages ago.'

'When?'

'I can't remember. Last year.' He handed the paper impatiently back.

'The ink doesn't look old to me.'

'What are you getting at?'

'Only the truth.'

160

He turned his frown on me, his eyes black in the sun. 'Look, Mike, you're on the wrong station. I'm not used to being called a liar.'

'This note has been written since February. It was in the pocket of a frock she didn't even have then. How often have you been seeing Lynn?'

He began moving again. 'Why the hell shouldn't I see her? We were friends at one time before you made this move—remember? Or has that conveniently escaped your notice since you became so much the boss?'

I said angrily: 'You damned fool, I had to make the move when I did—we were dying of strangulation in the old works—you know it as well as I do! And where you're concerned there's never been any more question here than at the other place of my being boss. As for friendship, I thought you were my friend as well as Lynn's!'

We came to the end of the tarmac and after a few seconds turned back.

I said: 'When did you write this note?'

'Four or five weeks ago. Sometime in early July.'

'Have you ever been Lynn's lover?'

That stopped him again. He looked at me with contempt and then gave a short laugh. 'You're a little out of your mind this afternoon.'

'That may be.'

'The answer's no. I haven't been Lynn's lover. But if you want the bare offensive truth, I gladly will be any time she gives me the opportunity!'

'She's not likely to now.'

'She never was likely to. More's the pity.'

I said: 'Why did you send this note?'

'She wrote and asked me to meet her in Letherton. I did. I met her several times. Any objections?'

'Why particularly did she want to see you then?'

He took out a packet of cigarettes but it was empty. I offered him one of mine but he shook his head and fished a half-smoked cigarette out of a matchbox.

'Was it to discuss my awful behaviour?'

161

'You admit it's been bad, then.'

'She'd reason to feel neglected, certainly.'

He lit a match and put it to the tattered end of the cigarette. The loose edges of the paper flickered into flame before the tobacco caught. He flipped the match away.

'Did she tell you I was having an affair with Stella Curtis?'

'There's not much point in being coy about it, is there?'

'Do you think it's true?'

'Well . . . pardon my disbelief . . .'

I put my hand on his coat. 'Did you think so before Lynn told you?'

He frowned again. 'I think so now.'

'*What* did Lynn tell you, Frank? Did she go into any sort of detail? It's vitally important I should know.'

He shrugged. 'Oh, God, what's the good of this? If you feel happier denying it all . . .'

'So far you've given me nothing specific to deny.'

'Oh, I can't remember what she told me. Anyway, she no doubt had it all out with you before she left. Personally it's none of my business, but I didn't think it very pretty taking the Curtis girl back to Greencroft when Lynn was out and playing ducks and drakes with her in your own home.'

'It might not have been pretty if it had ever happened.'

He hesitated and chewed the cigarette. 'And did Mrs. Thing, your housekeeper, imagine what she saw?'

'Mrs. Lloyd? What did she see?'

'Look, I'm not briefed for either of you——'

'Frank!'

After a minute he said: 'According to Lynn, so far as I can remember, you arrived at Greencroft with Stella Curtis one lunch-time—were annoyed to find Mrs. Lloyd still there and sent her packing. So Mrs. Lloyd being quizzy tiptoed back ten minutes later and looked in at the french windows and saw you'd got the girl on the settee. If it——'

'Just a minute.' I'd taken out a cigarette of my own but had waited to light it. Now I lit it. I was surprised to see the

162

flame of the lighter wobbling. 'Dear Mrs. Lloyd. So that's what she thought.'

'That's what she thought.'

'I remember the time she means. I'd brought Stella back to the house from Harwell, to pick up your IDA plans. When she got in the house she nearly fainted and had to lie down. I remember bending over her to give her a glass of brandy, and I believe I lifted her legs on to the settee. I suppose Mrs. Lloyd chose that moment to look in. It's surprising what a little imagination can do. Anything else?'

There was silence. Dawson said uncomfortably: 'What about last week when you conveniently got fogged up and spent the night at Brecon?'

'Lynn left me before that happened. I want to know what else *she* told you.'

'Oh, that you were with the Curtis girl all the time, that you were out at nights with her and cared nothing for your wife any more.'

'Was she asking your help in some way?'

His thin face flushed up again. 'Yes.'

'And you helped her?'

'If it's of any interest, no. She's had no direct evidence from me.'

'Could she have had any?'

'I don't know. You were always *with* Stella Curtis, weren't you? But spying isn't my line. When a fat little pus-head of a private detective came snooping round I told him to clear out.'

'Thank you at least for that.'

'Thank me for nothing. Now have you finished?'

'Did you tell Lynn you weren't prepared to help her?'

'Yes, eventually. She didn't like it much, and that's the last time I saw her.'

We'd been walking slowly back towards the buildings and now were less than fifty yards away. Thurston and Holborn had come out and were walking towards us.

I said: 'Did it occur to you, Frank, that Lynn might really be in love with somebody else and be trying to collect false evidence against me so that she could get her divorce the right way round?'

'No,' he said. 'I happen to be her friend as well as yours.'

The plane wasn't ready until seven. I went up in her first for a trial run, and then Holborn went up with Rhodes. I knew that on his report depended not merely whether they should install a radioaltimeter and use a bigger plane but whether they should use our equipment in its entirety or his. On it too might depend the future development of the factory, even possibly its survival. But also more important things than that.

About eight Dr. Bennett took me aside. He said: 'Always supposing that Holborn's report is not unfavourable, Mr. Granville; always supposing we decide to go ahead and ship your equipment as fitted, for use at once in the desert— is there any chance at all that you would be able to go with it?'

I stared at him. 'With it? D'you mean to operate it?'

'Yes. I've been talking the matter over with Porter. He feels very strongly that we can't afford any slip-up in operation. In spite of the claim that this equipment can be operated by non-technical people, the man who uses it must be skilled in the interpretation of the results. And it would be of immense benefit if there were someone there who understood it thoroughly in case of a breakdown. No one knows an instrument like its maker.'

'Thank you, Dr. Bennett. Unfortunately I have a factory.'

'And no one who could deputise?'

'I'm afraid not.'

'It would be interesting work, and would be completed in a few months. It might even be dangerous.'

'Do you tell me that as an inducement?'

He smiled. 'On the whole I thought you would have found it so.'

I said: 'I have—other problems as well.'

'It's a pity, because if the decision is a narrow one, the question of operator might influence us in making it. One hesitates sometimes over the unproven instrument, however promising it may seem in trials.'

'*I'm* sorry.' I stared out of the window at the blue of the evening sky over the hills. 'Anyway, Holborn's report may be highly favourable.'

At that moment Thurston came along the corridor. 'Oh, you're wanted on the phone, Granville. Somebody in London.'

'In London? Did they say who it was?'

'It's a man. I think he said Heppelwhite. Simon Heppelwhite.'

22

It was an ordinary telephone booth, a relic of the aerodrome days. I squeezed in and shut the door. 'Hullo?'

'Hullo. Michael?'

'Yes?'

'Oh, this is Simon.'

'Yes? Go on.'

'I may say I'm sorry to trouble you, but it happens we have here a visitor who says he's a friend of yours. I'm personally not at all sure whether he's a brilliant man or a lunatic. He says he has your authority to inquire into Lynn's sex life. Why he should come to see me . . .'

'What's his name?'

Simon lisped something but the phone crackled madly.

'What?' I shouted. 'What's his name?'

'Curtis. John Curtis.'

'Where are you speaking from?'

'My place in London.'

I stared at the phone. 'But you can't be—Curtis is a sick man. He's been in bed off and on for weeks. How has it——?'

'Is that what's the matter? You know him, then?'

165

'I know him but I don't understand how he's got up to London. Is he a tall, thin man in his middle forties with very clear deep-set brown eyes?'

'Yes, that's the fellow. It's not a mental thing he's had wrong with him, I hope?'

'Anything but . . . *What* does he want?'

'He wants to know all I know about Lynn. He says he has your authority to ask these questions. I can't quite understand why he should come to me. You do happen to be her husband!'

The mirror at the back of the phone was cracked. It made me look as if my eyes met over the bridge of my nose. I said: 'He already knows all I can tell him.'

'Well, what's it all about? Is he a private detective? I've never seen anyone less like one.'

'He's just a friend, Simon.'

'Helping you to collect evidence for a divorce?'

'No, not even that. I'm—very much with my head in a mousetrap just at this moment, and anybody . . . What does he want to know?'

'Details of her past life. Among other things, whether I'd call her a nymphomaniac. If he——'

'And would you?'

'What?'

'Would you call her that?'

There was silence while the three pips went.

He said: 'No, I should not. And I should have thought I knew her pretty well. But who am I to instruct her husband?'

'Well, instruct Curtis. He won't put it to any ill use.'

'Michael.'

'Yes?'

'The police were round yesterday asking about Lynn. Apparently she has taken it upon herself to disappear, not merely from you but from everybody.'

'Yes.'

'I don't think I should worry too much. Lynn has always had a flair for the dramatic. She'll very likely wait until it

166

gets in the papers and then make a terrific reappearance somewhere.'

I said: 'That's highly probable.'

'You speak feelingly, I'm afraid.'

'Where is Curtis now?'

'In the next room talking to Joy Fraser.'

It was on my tongue to tell Simon to keep his red-head out of this, but I didn't. I thought, well, what does it matter, in another day or so Lynn's private life will be front page news.

'Has Curtis got his wife with him?'

'No. I think he came by taxi.'

'Well, if he's not careful he'll . . .' I stopped; a sudden thought had got itself into my mind. I tried to finish the sentence but couldn't.

'Hullo.'

'Hullo. . . . Simon, will you give John Curtis a message for me?'

'Yes?'

'Tell him that nothing he does to help me—*nothing at all*—will justify him taking risks with his own life. Tell him . . . yes, tell him that you don't ever solve an equation by cheating, by—by striking out one of the principal symbols. Tell him——'

'Michael, I'm not a tape-recorder! I'll do my best, but make the rest of the message short.'

'No,' I said. 'That's all.'

I banged the receiver down and came out and stood staring at the tattered announcements on the notice-board. The oldest was an advertisement for a concert in Aberystwyth in March 1946. I was fogged and vexed and upset by John Curtis's move. There was no way he could help me by pestering my friends, nothing he could do that the police wouldn't do better; in fact it went dead counter to his own advice to me. I couldn't understand how Stella had allowed him to go, how he had got there. . . . I wished now I'd spoken to him direct. I wished very much that he hadn't gone.

Nothing that happened ever shaped towards understanding or relief. Frank Dawson had cleared up a few points of technical interest but had done nothing to help with the bigger things. John Curtis's rash, lunatic excursion couldn't help any more. It seemed to me it could have only one purpose. . . .

By now dusk was falling and the plane was not yet home. I went back into the phone booth and put through a call to Raglan Cottage. There was five minutes' delay but I wouldn't ring off, and stood in the box trying to overcome the feeling of hopelessness that had got me round the throat.

Someone had drawn chorus girls with large busts on the back wall of the phone booth. They all had the same upturned nose and the same vacant grin.

As I waited I heard the drone of the plane, and then I saw Thurston and Dawson go along the corridor towards the outer door. Neither of them saw me. There was a pause and then Rhodes and Holborn came in, accompanied by the other two, Rhodes taking off his flying jacket and apparently doing most of the talking. I caught sight of Holborn's face and thought it looked more bony and taciturn than ever.

'The phone's been ringing,' said the operator. 'Just a minute, I'll try them on another line.'

From where I was standing I could see the door of the room where we had our conference, and I saw Steel go in and then Bennett, and finally Porter and his secretary. After a minute Frank Dawson came out and looked up and down, then he saw me and came across and opened the door of the booth.

'Holborn's back. They're all waiting for you.'

'I know. Let them wait.'

He shoved back his black hair. 'Have it as you please. I thought you might be mildly interested.'

'I'll be there in five minutes.'

As the door of the booth shut I heard the operator give the number to the London exchange again. Dawson went limping angrily back. In a minute I heard the phone ringing in Raglan Cottage. It went patiently on, twenty-one times. Then the operator said: 'I'm sorry, there's no reply.'

'Thank you.' I hung up and came out. It had been hot in the booth and short of air. I decided I was feeling a bit queer. Perhaps it was one thing on top of another. Perhaps it was because I'd only had six hours' sleep since I found Lynn.

I went to the room and lit a cigarette before I opened the door. Then I changed my mind and put the cigarette out.

They were all sitting around waiting for me, but they'd all been talking about it before I came in; I could see by their faces. I came to my seat at the table and sat in it. Holborn was playing with his pencil again. Dr. Steel was polishing his glasses, Rhodes stroking the end of his moustache, the others were still.

I said: 'I was afraid you wouldn't get back before dark.'

Rhodes said: 'We've got non-radioactive phosphors on the panel now. All modern conveniences, as it were.'

Holborn glanced at Bennett. Bennett said: 'Mr. Holborn was just about to give us his report, Mr. Granville.'

I didn't speak but stared across at nothing.

Holborn said: 'I was explaining that "report" was too imposing a word for anything I can say after only ninety minutes' flying. You need time and varied circumstances to be able to make a thorough test. But of course I can give you my impressions, and I can link them, as it were, with the reports of the tests you have made this week and which I've studied fairly carefully to-day.' He still didn't look up but began to draw his figure eights again. 'My impression is that this survey instrument—in despite of its simplicity—to some extent because of it—is an advance on any other machine yet built. On its present showing and for its present purpose, I wouldn't alter it or add to it in any way.'

I didn't go back to London that night. The meeting didn't break up until twenty-five to ten, and then it became a smaller party of Thurston, Holborn, Rhodes, Dawson and me. Porter and Bennett and Steel all left, but the others were staying the night. I still felt under the weather and couldn't face the thought of a four- or five-hour drive through the night. Also the Old Bull didn't have a night porter and it would have meant knocking them up about three in the morning.

I knew that at some future time I should probably be happy about the results of to-day. I didn't regret having come and the personal risk of the further delay. There was a sort of dichotomy in my feelings at present that wouldn't let me have any satisfaction out of this result and yet didn't let me forget it.

I finally left Thurston and Holborn together talking like lovers—which they were, not of each other but of the things they were talking about. I'd borrowed an alarm clock and set it for five o'clock. The roads would be clear at six.

In bed I remember being very restless at first, trying to reason out how John had found the stamina to make a visit to London. I remember feeling certain there was something in what Simon had said to me that was pretty important and after a while my mind centred on that, turning over the conversation as often as I turned over in bed. Then suddenly it was daylight and I sat up rather scared thinking someone had switched on the light. I had slept through the alarm and it was ten minutes to seven.

I got up in a hurry, scraped some beard off with a borrowed razor and went hastily out to breakfast. There was only Frank Dawson at the long table.

I sat down nearly opposite him and he looked at me, half sardonic, half hostile, hunched a shoulder and went on with his breakfast. The one orderly came out and served me and we ate in silence. Physically I was feeling better.

I said: 'I'm sorry I can't take you back with me this morning, Frank. I've got to see a lawyer in London and I'm driving straight in.'

'I can cadge a lift from one of the others,' he said shortly.

Another silence fell. It was a fine morning but the sky had that brushed-over unpromising look.

He said: 'The scintillometer turned up trumps last night.'

'So did Holborn. I was afraid he was going to crab it.'

'He couldn't on its showing. Anyway he's far too honest.'

I looked at Dawson. 'Yes . . . I suppose I knew that all

along, but my judgment has got pulled out of shape these last few days.'

'Was that why you made such a wild-cat attack on me?'

I said carefully: 'They want a man to go out with the plane when it's shipped to Africa. They asked me but I can't go. I wondered if it would appeal to you.'

He looked at me curiously, assessingly. After a minute he shook his head. 'No, there's no point in me going. They want the brains out there or nothing.'

'You know a lot more about it than most people.'

He buttered a corner of toast and put it in his mouth. 'But a lot less than you.'

We didn't talk any more after that, but I finished quickly and went out to my car. None of the others seemed to be up yet. There was quite a strong wind blowing in from the west and the Auster had been run into one of the old hangars.

I threw my mack into the back seat and then remembered the brief-case I'd brought, and went back to the bedroom for it. As I came out into the corridor Frank was standing there plucking at his lip. He glowered at me.

'Look, Mike, I don't think I've played quite fair with you. I didn't tell you the whole truth last night.'

'About—Lynn?'

'About Lynn—and other things. You said did it seem to me that she might be in love with someone else and trying to collect evidence to use against you, and I said no. Well, that's true up to a point.'

'Oh?'

He hesitated. 'It's true up to about a month ago. But I happened to go into the Leather Jacket at Heaton Corner one Friday about seven and she was in there with a man. You don't need to have it down in black and white when she looked at him the way she did. They didn't see me so I got out fairly quick. . . .' Dawson shoved his hair back irritably.

I said: 'What was he like, this man?'

'Youngish, round face, looked as if he'd just come out of a bath. . . . Slick hair, Savile Row, breezy laugh. . . .'

'*When* was this?'

171

'Oh, it would be early last month. Let's see, the Monday I saw her last was the Monday when you had that flap about the condenser and worked on till midnight.'

'That was the thirteenth of July,' I said.

'Could be. Well, it would be the Friday before that.'

'The tenth. Two days after my visit to Glyndebourne.'

'What?'

'Did they seem—all right together, Lynn and this man?'

He stood with a finger inside his collar, moving it round as if it was too tight. 'I told you. I only watched them for a minute or two. Come to think of it, she seemed to be making the running. On the Monday following, as I say, I met her for a drink, and though I didn't say it out she must have guessed I'd rumbled something, and in the end because I wouldn't play ball she accused me of being disloyal to her. It's lovely the way women use the word loyalty, isn't it?'

'Have you been seeing Lynn more than you told me?'

'We've met ever since the factory moved—once or twice a month, I suppose. I—she started complaining almost at once.'

'Is that why you've been rather gunning for me ever since we moved?'

He flushed. 'Well—if I have—it's been that and maybe a guilty conscience. Read and I were equally to blame for that muck-up in February, and it's easy to ease your own mind by shoving the responsibility on someone else. Perhaps if I hadn't been so sore I wouldn't have believed all her stories. . . .'

Some seagulls were wheeling and crying in the early sunshine outside. A number of things seemed clearer to me this morning than they had done last night. I said: 'Perhaps it's a mistake to think too badly of Lynn, Frank. She never could help using her charm on people; it was the way she was made. But I think this once she got caught by it, by something in her own nature, and by something rather similar in another person. So in her distress she put to whatever use she could those of her friends who were in any

172

shape to help her. You were one of them. Mrs. Lloyd perhaps was another.'

He didn't seem to notice I had used the past tense. 'Do you know who the man is?'

'I have an idea. You haven't seen her at all since then?'

'No. I rang her a couple of times, because we didn't part too rosily and I didn't want to break with her altogether. The first time she seemed friendly again; but the second time she appeared to be having a row with someone and cut me off pretty short.'

'A *row*? What day was that?'

He shrugged. 'It isn't that important, is it?'

'Try to remember.'

He stared at me curiously.

'It would be the Wednesday or the Thursday.... The Thursday, because it was the first day that man came from R.R.E. to doctor the navigational computer. I rang her while you were with him—about three-thirty.'

'What did she say?'

'Not much. I phoned her and she answered and was talking to someone else while she picked up the phone, and then she snapped at me, and after a minute we hung up.'

I ran my tongue over my lips to make them less dry. 'Do you know if it was a man or a woman she was talking to?'

'Oh, I couldn't tell. But usually Lynn gets angry with men, doesn't she?'

'Walk with me to the car,' I said.

We went out.

I said: 'Can you remember *exactly* what she said, whether she made any excuse for cutting you off sharply, *how* she sounded angry? This may be absolutely vital to me, Frank.'

'I don't see what's vital about it.'

'I want to know who she quarrelled with that day.'

We got to the car. 'Actually she did say something before she answered me on the phone, like finishing the tail-end of what she'd been saying, d'you see? Flowers or Towers. Could that be his name?'

'No.'

'She sounded pretty mad. D'you remember when her cat was run over in London? A bit like that.'

'Did she just say the word "Flowers"?'

'No. I think she said, "What are you going to do, live with Flowers?" Or it could have been "live at the Towers". And then angrily into the phone, "Hullo!" She sounded to me near hysterics, so after a word or two I shut off. As a matter of fact, you were pretty short yourself later that night.'

I didn't get into the car. I stood staring at the old hangars. 'Frank, is there a London Telephone Directory in this place, do you know?'

'I haven't seen one. Why?'

'Let's go and look.'

We went and looked. We searched around in all the old cupboards and drawers.

'What d'you want it for?' Dawson said.

'Just a hunch. I'll try again when I get nearer home.'

We walked back to the car. I said: 'Frank, I've got to tell you. Something's cropped up that I can't explain. It may be days—perhaps *much* longer—before I get in to the works again.'

'Something I've told you?'

'No. But it's tied up with Lynn. You'll have to manage as best you can.'

'If there's a strike perhaps there won't be much to manage.'

'There can't be a strike. We can't afford it. It may be decided by now—but in any case it's up to you and Read to find a way out.'

'Read . . . ?'

'Yes, Read. Because from now on—if I shouldn't be there—you've got to try to get on with him. You've *got* to. Otherwise we'll be in the receiver's hands.'

He stared at me, wanting to fight but perhaps seeing in time that he must fight only himself.

'It'll be hard.'

'Well, let it be hard.'

I put out my hand and after a second he took it. 'O.K., Mike, if it comes to that I'll do my best.'

As I left the aerodrome a car passed me turning in.

I was in Brecon just before half-past eight and in Gloucester as the cathedral bells were ringing for ten o'clock. I stopped there for petrol and bought a paper and walked along to one of the hotels to see if they had a directory. They produced one of the old two-volume jobs, and I began to turn the pages of the C's.

Nothing under the C's. I tried the D's. De, Do, Dr., Du. . . . Du Caine. There were four Du Canes but only one spelling the name with an i, The Hon. Mrs. Charles du Caine. She had two numbers. One was for a Knightsbridge flat, the other was for The Towers, Epsom.

I put the phone books back and thanked the girl at the reception desk and walked slowly down the empty gusty street to my car. The bells had stopped. Those who were not in church were worshipping at their Sunday newspapers. I sat in the car and reached for a cigarette but I was out of them, so I just sat. Was that what Lynn had said? I sat for about ten minutes chewing at the end of my thumb. Then I got out again and went back to the hotel. I rang Letherton 407.

Stella answered.

I said: 'Darling. This is Mike.'

There was silence for a few moments. 'Hullo.' She sounded queer.

'Is John back?'

'Yes . . . last night.'

'Is he there? Is it possible to speak to him?'

'. . . No, I'm afraid not. Oh, Mike, why didn't you tell me?'

'About . . . ?'

'Yes, about her.'

'I was scared.'

'What of?'

'Of seeing disbelief in your eyes.'

175

'Oh, you *fool!* As if there could ever be that—about such a thing. Whatever else——'

'Thank you.'

'Where are you phoning from? No, don't tell me.'

'Why? I'm on my way home——'

'No, don't say. It may be that . . .' She didn't finish.

'What got into John last night? Why on *earth* did he go to London?'

'He gave me the slip, came back by taxi about midnight.'

'Is he all right?'

'Not too good.'

'Stella, what is it?'

'He collapsed about five this morning.'

'I'll come at once.'

'No, Mike! No. Hullo!'

'Hullo.'

'Don't ring off for a moment. And don't come here. John gave me a message for you. He woke me about half-past four—he said: "If Mike rings, tell him the wedding has to be stopped!"'

'The—wedding?'

'Yes. Does it make sense?'

I stared at the telephone. 'It's coming to make sense. But I don't know how John knows.'

'He said, "Tell Mike it's up to him."'

'Why shouldn't I come to see you?'

'I must go. There's someone at the door. Have you—read your Sunday papers?'

'No.'

Words came suddenly, hurriedly. 'I must go, Mike. Good luck, my darling. Take care.'

I said: 'Stella, what about John? What does——? Hullo! Hullo!' But she had rung off.

Once again I walked back to the car. Stop the wedding, John said. Ray French was marrying Margot du Caine at three this afternoon. I had the invitation in my pocket. 'What are you going to do, live at The Towers?' What

176

were the legal consequences of marriage? That a wife or a husband couldn't be called in evidence against the other?

I looked at my watch. A little over four hours yet. But there was no legal way to stop a perfectly legal wedding.

And what had Stella meant by all her hints and guarded allusions, as if she thought someone might be listening on the phone?

I got back to the car and opened the Sunday paper. At first there didn't seem anything of importance to me, except a column headed 'Torit Massacre'. The N.U.R. had put in a new wage claim with a threat of strike action if it wasn't met. An Egyptian had swum the Channel both ways. And then I saw it at the bottom of the front page. It was quite a short paragraph but was headed in strong black type: 'Girl's Body Found in Cellar.'

23

Sometimes you go hot like that when the doctor is stitching up a cut or the dentist's drill goes on too long.

'Acting on information received, the police this evening entered a house at Hockbridge (Beds.) and found in the cellar the body of a woman believed to be Mrs. Lindsey Granville, 27, the wife of the owner. Mrs. Granville has been missing three weeks, and inquiries have been proceeding for some time. A police officer declined to comment on the likely cause of death. Mr. Michael Granville, husband of the deceased, factory owner and top-rank radar expert, has not yet been interviewed.'

I'd clung to the safety-valve too long. I might have expected it. Sergeant Baker hadn't looked like a man who spent his time growing roses.

Mr. Michael Granville had not yet been interviewed. If that car turning in at the aerodrome was what I now thought it to be, it was by a matter of about ninety seconds that he had not been interviewed. . . .

I glanced over my shoulder but it was only two women coming down the street.

I started the car and accelerated away through the quiet town. The police would have my number now and a description of the car. I didn't know how these things worked. Was I now so badly wanted that they would stop me on the road, or did they reserve that sort of high pressure stuff for escaped bank raiders?

Don't take the most direct route to London anyway; if anything they'll watch the Oxford Road. At Witney fork left for Bicester and Aylesbury.

I could imagine Greencroft now, the reporters, the unemotional police, the whispering peering people outside; and inside the professional activity, the technical expertise that as a technical man myself I ought to be able to appreciate. By now they'd have taken *her* away. By now Mrs. Lloyd would have made her statement. The quarrels we'd had, the way I'd been carrying on in my own house with another woman, she'd seen it with her own eyes, the way I'd been reluctant to open the door to her that first morning. Mrs. Granville's gone away, he'd said, to look after her mother; she won't be back for some time. By now the police would have been to see Stella. Tell me, Mrs. Curtis, how long have you known Mr. Granville? How often have you been to his home since Mrs. Granville disappeared?

And John Curtis was dying. Was that what Stella had said over the phone? You couldn't get away from what it added up to. 'What,' I'd said to him, 'would you do if you found out the things in this petition were true?' And he'd answered, 'Take steps to remove myself from the scene.' Guessing by now, perhaps, about Stella, he'd reasoned that after all he didn't need the gas fire. There was an easier way. And what more suitable than to kill himself helping the man who'd taken his wife?

Wasn't that following the code of conduct that he lived by? Wasn't it true to his ideals that he should squander his failing vitality in some forlorn hope helping a worthless selfseeker like me?

I stopped a couple of miles from Aylesbury and found a crumpled cigarette in the cubby-hole and smoked that. Three hours yet. What did the self-seeker do now?

John expected me to tackle Ray French in some way, either through Digby Hamilton or on my own. He expected me to put a stop to a wedding designed to prevent the police from coming at evidence which would clear me. How John had come to that conclusion I hadn't the faintest idea, but after what Frank had told me I was sure he was right. I knew who had been in the room at Greencroft on the afternoon Lynn died, and presumably Margot du Caine knew too. Somehow in the next three hours I had to devise some means of stopping Ray French from marrying her, even if it meant tackling him in his flat and tying him up and locking the door. A delay in the wedding for even twenty-four hours might give time for the saving moves to be made.

While John Curtis quietly died in Letherton. That was it, wasn't it? It was all laid out on a plate for me. I saved myself and he bled to death. As simple as that.

I chucked the cigarette away. It was faintly flavoured with something, and I saw that an old lipstick of Lynn's had been rolling against it in the cubby-hole. I started up the car. After about five miles I turned left again, away from London and towards Letherton.

The cottage might be watched. Stella was the woman in the case, and the police would expect me to turn up there. But a wood came down behind the cottage at the back, and a narrow lane, beginning at the Cock and Pheasant half a mile away, wound round to the other side of the wood. I took that.

About thirty yards separated the wood from the cottage, and at the last tree I took a good look round. No one. Smoke came from the chimney of the cottage, and upstairs the curtains were part drawn as if to keep out the light. Not that there was much light, because heavy clouds had blown up.

179

I jumped over the hedge and made across the grass. I didn't bother to knock. Stella was in the kitchen.

'Mike!' She stared at me with huge dark-shadowed eyes.

'Are you alone?'

'At present. Except for John. I came down to refill his bottles. But if——'

'How is he?'

'He came round about nine. Mike, why ever did you come here when——?'

'How did he get up to London last night?'

A bit startled by the way I said it, she told me. '. . . I couldn't think why he wanted the soda water. When I got back he wasn't here; only a note. He came back at midnight—didn't seem much worse at first—even though he's not been out of the cottage for weeks.'

'And then?'

'The police have been here, asking—— Did anyone see you come in?'

'I don't think so——'

'Darling, what a *terrible* thing; when John told me . . . Who killed her, Mike?'

I said: 'Tell me about John.'

The kettle was boiling and she switched it off.

'A hæmorrhage about five. Dr. Lewis wanted to get him to hospital but he was too weak. They gave him a blood transfusion here at seven. We couldn't get a nurse but the District Nurse came in for a couple of hours. She'd just gone when the police came. . . .'

'What did they want to know?'

She began to fill the bottle. It was queer standing here in this cottage kitchen on a domestic chore. Her lashes were very dark on her face when it was as pale as this. '. . . And they thought I might know where you were. I choked them off—made the excuse that John . . . They're coming back later.'

'What chance is there now for him?'

'Dr. Lewis didn't say much. This—this is the way people die of this complaint. But he's been better since about eleven.'

'Can I go and see him?'

'Yes. Yes, for a few minutes. Can you tighten this screw?'

I took the bottle from her. 'Did he tell you where he'd been last night?'

'Enough for me to know you ought to be in London now.'

We looked at each other. Then she turned to fill the other bottle.

'What did he tell you?' I said.

'He says he reasoned it out. This man you spoke of, Ray French, told you that Lynn was a nymphomaniac, didn't he?'

'Well?'

'Well, John apparently reasoned that Ray French couldn't be mistaken. That is, he couldn't be *wrong*. Either he was right or he was lying.'

'Yes, I see that.'

'Then he thought, *you* didn't think she was a nymphomaniac, but you might be deceived. Who else might know? The best chance was Simon Heppelwhite, who, you told him, had employed Lynn for some years and who had been a great friend of hers. He thought Simon Heppelwhite might have views on the subject.'

Too much steam had got into the bottle and it suddenly bubbled and spat hot water. She held it away from the kettle.

'And what did Simon say?'

'He said no. He said, to talk of nymphomania was nonsense. He'd known about Lynn and Ray French for months, and had quarrelled with Lynn about it, for letting you down. She was mad over Ray French; no one else.'

I took the second bottle from her. 'And then?'

As I spoke there was the sound of a heavy fall overhead.

Stella had been going to refill the kettle, but now she dropped it and fled up the stairs, and I was close behind her.

We got in to see the bed empty and John sprawled upon the floor beside it. The whiteness of his skin when we rolled him over was nearly grey.

'John,' she said. '*John. . . .*'

181

He was breathing, but there was no pulse at all.

'Can you help me?' I said.

'Of course.'

I took his shoulders and she his feet. He seemed a terrific weight. Somehow we got him back on the bed.

'He said he'd be all right while I went downstairs. He must have tried to get out and fallen. . . .'

Now that he was back in a normal position his breath was coming in deep gasps, like a man drowning.

'The doctor left something,' Stella said, her lips trembling. 'If he fainted. That syringe. Cora something.'

'Coramine.' I picked up the syringe and held it up to the light. 'Shall I do it?'

'Please.'

I put the thing somehow into his arm and pressed it home. His skin was sweaty and cold.

'I'll get Dr. Lewis,' she said.

'Wait. I think he's coming round.'

Perhaps my clumsy puncture had roused him. His eyelids were fluttering. Stella moistened his lips, and suddenly I found him looking straight at me. Without a sound he said my name.

'John,' I said.

His eyes travelled to Stella. 'Sorry about that,' he muttered. 'Thought I could . . .'

'Don't talk.'

He shifted slightly. 'Used to believe—couldn't keep a good man down. Now I realise—only a relative statement.'

I made some sort of answer.

He frowned. 'You shouldn't be here, Mike. Time is it?'

'Plenty of time yet.'

'You—got my message?'

'Yes, it's all right. I'm going to act on it.'

His eyes closed then. I looked at Stella and nodded. She slid out of the room.

He'd gone off again. I felt for the pulse at the root of his neck; it was just there. On the table by the bed was a glass pot on a stand with a rubber tube and a filter, and a few other odds and ends. The light in here was distilled by the curtains, discreet and without shadows. I went to the window and looked out. The garden was empty.

She came back. 'He's not in, but they'll ring me as soon as they can find him.'

I nodded.

We were silent for a time. The drug was having a good effect on him, but he hadn't come round again.

She said: 'You *must* go, Mike.'

'Not yet.'

'What time is the wedding?'

'There's time.'

'How can you stop it? Can you see Digby Hamilton?'

I said: 'What else did John tell you about last night?'

'He went to see Margot du Caine.'

"What?"

"I'm only telling you what he told me. There was a girl there with Simon Heppelwhite. I've forgotten her name——'

'Joy Fraser.'

'Yes. She knows Margot du Caine and is going to her wedding to-day. I don't know how much John told Joy Fraser or what she said, but it came out that Ray French had been making a great attempt to get the wedding put forward. A week ago he almost had a row with everyone concerned, and at last Margot agreed to get married by licence this Sunday.'

'I still don't see why John . . .'

'He said, if Ray French were innocent, the haste to get married to *that* extent was hard to understand. If he were guilty, and he was sure he was, then the haste was simple to explain. You only had to look on Margot as an accessory, especially if she was an innocent one. . . . I don't know what he said to Joy Fraser, but whatever he said must have impressed her, because she took him straight along to the du Caine's flat and introduced him.'

'And then?'

'He talked to the girl and to her mother. Again I don't

know what he said, but whatever he tried didn't come off. They wouldn't believe him.'

The man on the bed stirred and she was across to him instantly. But he made no other move.

I went to peer out of the window again, and she came back.

'You've got to go, Mike.'

'Not while I can be of help.'

'You certainly have been.'

'And I want to know why he went off as he did last night.'

I think she saw what I meant.

'He wanted to help you and did help you without considering the cost to himself.'

'Aren't I allowed the same luxury in return?'

'*No*. . . . Because you both do it at my expense!'

That held me for a bit. I said: 'I hadn't thought of it that way. Maybe I need even more egoism than I've got to see it that way.'

'Or less pride.'

I looked at her. Physically she was as close to me now as at any time since last Sunday. I looked at the soft flare of her nostril, the fine skin under the dark curling hair beside her ear, the sheen of her eyelashes and the curve of her lips. Last Sunday. But we'd come such a long way since then.

A train went past. The line was some distance away but it caused a tiny vibration of two of the bottles on the table. As it stopped we heard the telephone ringing.

'I'll answer it,' she said.

It was raining now. My watch said five minutes to one.

'Mike,' said John.

I went quickly to him.

His lips moved when I came into his view. Some of the dead whiteness had gone. 'Heard you—mumbling there.'

'Sorry. We thought——'

'Stella been—telling you—my visit to Margot du Caine?'

'Yes.'

'Peculiar interview.'

'Don't talk now. Lewis is coming.'

184

He made a face. 'There was—no moving her, Mike. I could tell by the look in her eyes she knew *something*. My hunch was right. By marrying her, French is in some way covering up. But she pretended—didn't know what I was talking about. I told her—Lynn was dead. She said— unpardonable interference. Tried to show me the door. Her mother ... I appealed to her. I think—she thought me insane. But the girl did not. The girl did not.'

'You did your best.'

'Time is it?'

'Plenty of time yet.'

'It's—up to you, Mike. You've got to stop it.'

There was the sound of a car drawing up outside the cottage.

'John, I have to ask you one thing.'

He closed his eyes for a couple of seconds and then looked at me. 'Yes?'

'I want to know why you did that yesterday—getting up against all orders, nearly killing yourself.'

He gave a faint shrug. 'It looked to me—a fair and reasonable expenditure to make.'

I said: 'You know when the divorce petition came; I asked you, supposing what it said were true, what would you have done—and you said you'd take steps to remove your-self.'

'Yes?'

A door banged. I said hastily: 'Coming here I had the idea that perhaps you thought Stella was in love with me—why you should think that, God knows, but you apparently considered it possible on Friday. And that if you thought that, you might—have taken these steps.'

I watched him. He considered. 'Done it—to kill myself?'

'Yes.'

'It would be—roundabout way, wouldn't it?'

'I thought you might have considered it appropriate.'

'How?'

'Well, it might go with your ethics. Helping the man whom you thought ...'

185

He smiled and his gaze didn't flicker. 'I see you don't—understand me.'

'I'm sorry if I don't.'

'Or you underrate my—liking for you.'

'I don't understand *that*.'

There were voices downstairs.

'Nor would it—go with my ethics, as you call them.' He paused, listening, and then said quickly, with an effort: 'Wouldn't doing that, my doing that, have the opposite effect of what you think? Wouldn't that way be putting a barrier between you and Stella for ever?'

I stared at him and he stared back at me.

'Yes,' I said.

There were footsteps on the stairs. 'One is—not always detached, Mike. Don't make the mistake of thinking I am. I hate the misfortune that's come on me. But I don't hate you.'

I put my hands on his. 'I can't think of anything to say.'

He returned the pressure. 'Say nothing. But go.'

Stella and Dr. Lewis came into the room.

I waited downstairs. I knew it was cutting it impossibly fine now. An hour from here to Chelsea even on a Sunday afternoon. Fairly certainly so far as the wedding was concerned I'd lost the trick. But I didn't regret having come.

There were photographs in the room, one of Stella, one of a woman I didn't know. His first wife perhaps. If it was only as good of her as it was of Stella, I shouldn't get far by looking at it. I felt pressed down with a sense of not knowing, and a sense of fatality along with it. At the moment I was one making up a set of six. John and Stella, Lynn and Ray and Margot du Caine. I felt I didn't understand a thing about the motives or feelings of any of them, why passion blew up where it didn't belong, why loyalties and deceits had got tied in with crime and punishment. I could only guess at half the reasons behind what had happened, and I saw no hope at all that I would ever know more.

In about a quarter of an hour Stella came down.

186

'He's having another blood transfusion. Dr. Lewis says he's responded well to the first. I slipped down to tell you to go.'

'He'll be all right?'

'As right as he can be. Perhaps two weeks in bed. Then he *may* get up again. . . .'

I peered out again, at the garden and the rain.

'Now do you feel free?' she said, almost angrily.

'Yes, I feel free.'

It was a queer expression of the way I was at present fixed. I kissed her and left. This was the final good-bye and had to be excused.

I got across to the wood without any trouble. Fifty yards brought me to the edge of the lane. My car was where I had left it, and I was going to climb over the low wall and go towards it when some sort of sixth sense made me decide to have a look first from the other side. I ducked back into the wood and approached this time from about a hundred yards ahead. I didn't get very far. In a green-lichened gateway of the wood just out of sight of the car, and conveniently placed to step out at the right moment, a policeman was waiting.

24

I made for the station. Once out of the wood at the eastern corner, you were up against the raw new villas at the edge of the town; and from there it was only two hundred yards. I knew all the back streets of Letherton.

Of course they might be waiting for me, but that was a risk that had to be taken. There wasn't any other way of getting to London now.

There was a train in ten minutes. That was lucky for a Sunday, but it didn't alter the fact that it takes an hour and five minutes from Letherton to King's Cross, and from there I had to get to Chelsea.

It still didn't matter as much as it should have done. Even in practical terms my visit to the cottage hadn't been thrown away.

I didn't think I'd proved anything to anybody by going to see John Curtis, not even to myself, but at least I hadn't snapped at the bait that circumstances had shoved in my way. I'd behaved like a fool two or three times in the last few days, but this time at least I hadn't been trying to save myself. Perhaps it showed a twisted outlook, not being able to accept what he'd tried to do for me—but I couldn't, on those terms.

The train was five minutes late. I got on it all right and settled into the corner of a third-class carriage; there were two other men in the carriage; one in a blue mack nodded to me; doors slammed and the dirty, smoke-grey engine stammered on the greasy lines.

The man in the mack said something about the weather, and, finding he was speaking to me, I agreed, then they went on talking between themselves. They were going to some sort of a meeting, and the other chap, who was in black, was going for the first time.

We ran into the next station, a halt, oddly rural-looking, left over, an anachronism. As we waited there an express went through on the fast middle line; rattling windows, carriages flickering like a halting movie film.

We were off again. 'It's the following that's hard, d'you see,' said the man in the mack, biting his nails. 'Mr. Thompson always emphasises that with new members. The *following* and the *acceptance*. . . .'

The train was late. It was nearly three when we stopped at New Barnet, and from there on into a darkening city with the sky yellow and a heavy downpour settling in, the train crept forward as if scared of being checked at every signal. As we slid along the platform of King's Cross I opened the door of the carriage; a porter's face stared, passing. The man in the blue raincoat said:

'You'll get wet, sir, with no hat or coat. It's raining. Like to borrow my umbrella?'

I stared at him.

He said: 'It's got my name and address inside.'

'Thanks. Thank you. . . . No, I haven't far to go.'

I got out quickly and made down the platform, gave my ticket; no taxi waiting but I caught one in Euston Road. It was twenty past three. There might have been some delay.

'St. James's Church in Chelsea.'

'Eaton Place?'

'Yes.'

While we were on the way I took out once more the invitation to the wedding. The reception afterwards was at the Royal Hotel, which was in King's Road. Where the couple were spending the night I didn't know; he'd said they were to stay in London.

The afternoon traffic was just beginning, but the heavy rain kept people off the streets. Queues outside cinemas, and in Hyde Park a few tub-thumpers persevered to clusters of hardy listeners. He took the route down Grosvenor Place and turned left at Chapel Street. It was ten to four.

As we turned into Eaton Place there were no cars waiting and I knew it was all over. The taxi stopped outside the church and I got out. Bits of sodden confetti lay trampled in the rain. The church was dark and empty except for an old woman sitting in a pew in the lady chapel. A notice-board said that evensong was at six. I walked up as far as the altar and back. There was a nice show of flowers.

I went out to the taxi again and stood for a few seconds. A lunatic interruption at the wedding might have had some result. Nothing could come from breaking into the wedding luncheon. Nothing really could help now at all.

'If I was you, mate, I should get back in. You'll be drier there.'

'Drive me to a telephone box, will you.'

We purred round a couple of streets and into Belgrave Square. On the way I thought out a list of the ten best hotels.

I borrowed some change from the driver and began. When

189

the first one answered I asked to speak to Mr. Raymond French. After a pause the receptionist said: 'I'm sorry, sir, there's no one of that name staying in the hotel.' I tried five and got the same answer from each. At the sixth there was a longer pause, then the girl said: 'I'm sorry, there's no reply from the suite. If you'd care to wait I'll have him paged.' I said, No thank you, and rang off.

It was a hotel overlooking Hyde Park. I got back in the taxi and told him to drive me there.

I could wait. There was nothing more to lose now and I could wait.

I went into the tea lounge of the hotel, which was convenient for seeing people coming in and out of the revolving doors; and being Sunday it was quiet. After a while I began to feel dizzy and light-headed so I ordered tea. The waiter didn't think much of my looks but he only commented with his eyebrows, and went away and brought the tea. I sat and drank it and ate toast and cakes, and thought about things. A few well-dressed people were about now, talking in brittle, polished, crackly voices, but I didn't take my eyes off the doors. It was now a quarter to five. The police would be getting anxious about Mr. Michael Henry Granville, factory owner and top-rank radar expert, who had not yet been interviewed. Perhaps Mr. Michael Henry Granville was on the run.

'Calling Major Moolchan, calling Major Moolchan,' said a page boy in a green uniform with brass buttons. A tall well-dressed Indian with an anonymous sort of face got up at the end of the room and hurried out.

I paid my bill and went over to the book counter for some cigarettes. I'd not had any real desire to smoke for some hours, but one had to have something to do.

A woman there was arguing querulously with the man behind the counter. 'But I know it's been published, I saw it in Paris.' 'I'm sorry, madam, perhaps it was an American edition.' She'd been a pretty woman twenty years ago; all the gestures were still there, the rings flashing as the hand trembled up to the dyed hair. Her fine eyes went coquettishly over me and then she turned back to the assistant. 'Who are those for?' said a black-coated employee beside me. 'Four-two-six. Name of French.' 'Take this up with you, will you, give it to Ferguson of room service. Same floor.' 'O.K.'

I'd bought my cigarettes and paid for them before the words properly sank in. It had been a page boy who had answered the man, and he was walking away now with a box of orchids in his hands.

'But you must have *something* by him. I met him in Monte last year. There was a book of his mentioned in *Country Life,* I'm sure.'

'I'm sorry, madam, but there doesn't seem to be anything in print. These are the latest lists.'

The page boy had got into the lift. I stood and watched the doors close. A cigarette was unlit in my hand. I walked across to the lift on the opposite side of the foyer.

'Four-two-six,' I said to the attendant.

We went imperceptibly up. The attendant flashed his lighter for me but I shook my head. As the door slid open I said: 'Which way is it from here? I usually go up on the opposite side.'

'Turn to your right, sir, and then left at the end of the passage.'

I followed the directions. In the third passage a door was open. As I got near it the page boy was just coming out.

I said: 'Oh, have you brought something for me?'

He smiled. 'Yessir. Or I think perhaps it's for madam.'

'Good. Thank you.' I gave him half a crown.

I went in and the door closed behind me. Then I had time and breath to light the cigarette.

A drawing-room with french windows and a balcony, a lavender-blue bedroom, a bathroom leading off. The orchids said: 'To my darling Margaret from her adoring Ray.' It was like an obituary notice. Not much personal in the bedroom except one suit-case marked already with the trophies of travel: *"Hôtel Splendide, Deauville; Hôtel du*

Parc, Bruxelles.' On the bureau were a half-dozen labels neatly printed: *'French, S.S. Otrantes, Stateroom Baggage.'*

The hotel was very quiet. People went out of London on a summer week-end. The french windows were ajar and I closed them. A freckle of rain had been falling on the edge of the expensive cinnamon-coloured carpet. With the windows shut it was still quieter. There was a telephone in the drawing-room cunningly disguised in the writing bureau, and another phone by the bed. I went into the bedroom and hesitated and then lifted the receiver and asked the hotel operator to get me Letherton 407.

It took a little time to get through. I could hear the receptionist talking about Danny Kaye. Then a voice said: 'Letherton 407.'

'Darling,' I said. 'Stella, darling . . .'

'Mike, where are you?'

'Never mind. Have the police been again?'

'Yes, a few minutes after you left. Are you in London?'

'Yes. But they got my car.'

'So they told me. What about the wedding?'

'It went on. How's John?'

'Sleeping now. But Mike——'

'Don't worry about the wedding. Are the police still there?'

'Oh, no, they left soon after. They left as soon as they knew you'd gone. It was a man called Baker.'

'I know him.'

'John insisted on seeing him for a moment. Are Ray French and this girl——?'

'What did he say to the police? D'you know?'

'One thing, Mike, I must tell you. It was John who first told the police.'

'What? About what?'

'About Lynn being dead and where she was. I didn't know that until they came this afternoon.'

I said: 'I can't believe it. If he——'

'Well, listen. Apparently what he did was——'

192

I said: 'I'll have to ring off now. I'm sorry. I'll ring you again as soon as I can.'

'But Mike——'

I put the phone down. Ray French was standing in the doorway of the bedroom watching me.

25

Sometimes you wait for a moment, and when it comes you don't know what to do with it; the event has suddenly run back on itself, gone unmanageable. Imagination is swallowed by temperament.

He said: 'Don't bother about me, old boy. There's no need to cut it short on my account.'

I got up and picked my cigarette out of the ash-tray. 'I'm sorry I couldn't make the wedding.'

He shrugged. 'These affairs are never passionately interesting, are they, except to the people concerned.' He threw his gloves on the bed, passed a hand over his sleek hair, straightened his jacket with a brief downward tug of the hands behind the pockets.

'It wasn't lack of interest.'

'Well, I expect you had your plate pretty full, did you?'

'Full of what?'

His eyes came back from the mirror and went over me. There wasn't much expression on his face. It was like an empty house. 'I haven't seen the papers but somebody told me. Dear boy, what's been going on? Is Lynn really dead? I can't tell you how distressed I am.'

'She's dead,' I said. 'I really came along to ask you why you killed her.'

It might have been a stone, the question thrown at him like that. There was a flicker of dislike round the corners of his eyes and lips as he turned back into the drawing-room. I followed quickly, thinking he might be going to call some member of the hotel staff, but instead he went across to a table where there was a siphon and a glass.

'How thirsty marriage makes one! I'll ring down for some whisky——'

'Where's Margot?'

'Downstairs.'

I said: 'That night at Glyndebourne was the first time Lynn saw you with her, wasn't it? I thought she was raging at me that night, but really she was raging at you.'

He went to the french windows, opened them, stood frowning out at the day.

'I hope this strong wind drops before to-morrow. Margot's not at all a good sailor.'

I said: 'Doesn't it worry you that I may have to pay for a murder you committed?'

'It worries me that you may suffer,' he said over his shoulder. 'As your friend, that worries me madly. But *if* I had done what you say, the alternative would worry me more.' He sighed. 'Oh, well, that's what life's like. I'll get the whisky.'

He moved to go round me into the bedroom, but I got in his way. He smiled at me. It was a pretty queer smile.

'What is this, Mike—a hold-up?'

I said: 'I suppose what Lynn was hoping to do was manœuvre me into a position where I might agree to a divorce and a permanent settlement on her, a larger share of the partnership—not alimony which would stop if she married you. She loved you but she knew you had to be bought.'

There was no doubt that his good-fellowship was losing its brightness. Like a badge suddenly tarnished. 'And always supposing that was her aim, would you have done it?'

'Done what?'

'Agreed to settle a larger income on her without conditions?'

I screwed out my cigarette, felt the hot tobacco under my fingers. 'I suppose you thought you couldn't risk it. Was that it?'

'Always supposing that was the set-up, it would, I admit, have been a dubious point.'

I watched him. 'And then Margot came along, eh?'

'You tell me.' He had moved back into the drawing-room.

I said: 'I don't know why you went to see Lynn that last afternoon, and I don't know what part Margot took in it. But I think you'd probably been playing them both along until the last minute, and Lynn, having seen you with Margot and being full of anxiety, decided to bring things to a head by bullying her lawyer into filing a petition at once. Probably on the Thursday morning she phoned you to say, "Darling, I'm leaving Mike to-night and coming to the flat; can you meet me there?" That sort of thing? And you had the job of going round and telling her you were going to marry Margot after all.'

He had taken the carnation out of his button-hole and was sniffing it. The flower looked faded, and after a minute he crumpled the stem between his short, manicured pianist's fingers.

I said: 'Surely you didn't take Margot with you, to reason with this—nymphomaniac.'

He smiled and said: 'Lynn was an exciting woman, and usually you don't find women like her with a high standard of morals. But I really believe she'd been faithful to you until I came along. After that there was never anyone else in it at all.'

For the first time there was something in his voice. Some flickering memory . . .

I said: 'If you felt that way about her, why did you turn her down?'

'You've already arrived at the answer, my dear Mike. Money. Just money.'

In spite of his care he was talking. There was life after all in the empty house.

'When you're wealthy, old boy, it's easy to live on a lofty moral plane. You are in a well-paid racket. You get thousands of pounds for making repulsive little airborne computers which will enable as yet unweaned babies to be more skilfully and scientifically blinded and scalded to death. My racket is a badly-paid one. Except for a dozen at the top we artistic fools who make music may starve to death for all the public or the state cares. When I was in my teens, Mike, I used to practise at the piano seven and eight hours a day. I thought I was going to make a baker's dozen of the top twelve. But not so. I can play Beethoven and Schumann and Busoni with such technical expertise that in your profession I should more than get by. In my profession I don't quite get by. So I'm expected to rot in the gutter like an old banana skin.'

He bent his head, pulling bits of the flower off and sniffing them before dropping them on the floor. 'Not so again. I am quite unwilling to rot or to starve. I like the good things of life. I enjoy driving a fine motor-car just as much as you do. Caviare tastes as well on my lips; possibly I know more than you about a Latour 1934. So I've had to scrape the barrel and turn to use a gift for pleasing women. I'll give you a few tips sometime.'

'I understand a lot but I don't understand why you had to kill her.'

He was at last left with only the stalk of the white carnation in his fingers. It was already well broken and he began to nip off bits with his thumb-nail.

'My dear man, if you have any suspicions go and confide them to the police. It's perfectly obvious to me that you put her under the coals yourself.'

I said: 'Were you smiling when you dragged her into the cellar and shovelled coal over her?'

His eyes twitched. 'Was that how you did it?'

I said: 'Lynn was my wife, Ray. I know now I didn't love her or look after her as I should have done. I shall always blame myself for that. But she didn't deserve to be—broken like that, buried—you should have seen her, after three weeks.'

'You saw her?'

'I saw her.'

He stared at me and licked his lips.

The telephone in the bedroom began to whir.

I don't think he had noticed the phone in here because he

made a move towards the bedroom door. I got in his way again. 'I'll answer it,' I said.

'I'm sorry. You won't.'

I had turned to go into the bedroom myself but he gripped my arm. We looked at each other. I should have seen the danger. (But he'd won all along the line; he'd nothing to gain by pressing now.)

I shoved him away. He leaned back, dropping his hands, but before I could get into the bedroom he had grabbed my other arm, pulled me and himself three or four paces into the drawing-room. We stopped, breathing hard, hesitating on the edge of worse. The telephone went on.

He made a move to go round me, but I caught at him and we lurched against the wall, slid along it. There's a perverted intimacy about violence; I could smell the stuff of his suit, the cigarette smoke on his breath; this is what Lynn loved; and in loving perhaps learned to hate; another obligation on me? Perhaps I could pay off in the only currency left.

Anger suddenly caught at me, and I swung at his smooth clean face. Knuckles on it, pleasure in marking, in damaging. Suddenly his face changed, twisted, and he came for me with both hands; as I raised mine he kicked violently up at my knee. I lurched away and he followed and caught my flying arm, wrenched at it; I fell across his shoulder and was flung over it five feet across the room.

It was like being knocked out by an iron door. I had just sense and control to lie still, I could just see the hazy light from the window and his shadow standing over me. I thought he was going to kick me again, but the telephone which had been silent began again. He went out to it.

I rolled over and got to my knees and tried to lose the meal I hadn't eaten. Then I began to crawl towards the telephone in the writing-desk. I got to it but couldn't get up so had to pull the receiver off. Then I lay on the floor with my ear to it.

A cautious voice saying: '. . . fortunate to get you a seat on the twenty twenty-eight for Brussels. There happened to be just one seat left, sir.'

197

'That's Sabena?'

'Yes, sir. Leaving Waterloo at seven. Er—do I understand you'll not be occupying your suite to-night?'

'I shall not, but—er—my wife . . . She'll be along later, of course. She'll be here. But if you'll make out my account now . . .'

'Certainly, sir. Shall we send the air ticket up to you?'

'No, I'll collect it. Oh, and—er—will you see that the suite is *on no account* disturbed—until my wife comes, that is. I shall be leaving some private papers about. . . .'

'Of course, sir. I'll send up instructions at once.'

'Thank you.' There was a click.

I didn't bother to try to put the phone back. It took all I had to get to my feet. I got to my feet. I looked round for something handy and saw the soda siphon. I made across to it and picked it up. Ray came out of the bedroom and stood back against the door. His face was like a smart woman's when the make-up is taken off.

He said: 'Feeling ill? You pale lily-fingered scientists bending over a bench all day, you've got no guts. You should try being an artist for a few weeks, it would get you in condition.'

I didn't say anything. His glance strayed to the dangling telephone. After a pause he said: 'Murder's one of the rarer carnal experiences, isn't it? You can't qualify or divide it. And at the time perhaps you don't want to.'

The teeth were showing at last. I said: 'Why aren't you taking Margot with you?'

He walked over and slammed the telephone back on its rest. 'Have you ever seen Lynn in a temper—suddenly white hot, an electric wire short-circuiting. Have you? Has she ever come at you with her nails just like a cat, wanting your eyes out? What did you do in self-defence against the sweet girl? Did you fight Marquess of Queensberry? I was in the Commandos, my dear Mike, while you were hatching nasty eggs in your safe little back room. In the Commandos they teach you fascinating technical tricks of another kind. The only thing they don't teach you is

198

that some people's necks break easier than others. Lynn's must have been very flimsy. I let her go as soon as she dropped her claws.'

By moving to the telephone he had halved the distance between us. He said savagely: 'It was a hell of a way to hide her, but when it comes to the point you find that the corny place is the only place. I knew the police would look there.'

'Why did you come back the next night?'

'I'd left a gramophone catalogue that wasn't due to be published until the following week. What made you come here, now, to-day? How the hell did you get in here? What's put you on to me again?'

'Hasn't your marriage shut down on all the evidence you hoped it might?'

He wiped the back of his hand across his mouth, which was swelling at the corner. 'I'm not married, my dear Mike.'

We stared at each other. A clock somewhere was chiming the half-hour. He said: 'Was it some friend of yours who called in on Margot last night, told her Lynn had been murdered, shook her innocent faith in what I'd told her? Was it?'

'Yes.'

'She didn't believe him then but she rang me after. I pacified her, told her he was a madman. I think she believed me. But then the newspapers came to-day. . . . That settled it. I've just left her after three hours. She must have a week's postponement.' He looked at the siphon I held. 'She must have it. Well, she'd have been a dull woman to live with, dull after Lynn.'

He was leaning now with his hands on the back of a chair. I said: 'Then it's really you that's on the run.'

'Not yet. The mills of God. But now that you've pushed in . . . I hope your neck is stronger than hers.'

I said: 'Lynn was my wife.'

His eyes twitched again. 'She wasn't much good, you know, not at heart. But she was good in other ways. She'd no thought for *anyone* but me. Not a thought in her head or her body. Once before she scratched me with her nails, all

199

down my back, not in anger but in love. In love and passion. She was like a warm fish, with claws. Have you smelt o' the bud o' the briar or the nard i' the fire, or have tasted the bag o' the bee? She was a soft white bitch and her neck broke like chalk in my hands. Christ, it broke like chalk, and she was dead—just in ten seconds. I thought she'd fainted till the colour changed, changed while I was still holding her. Her eyes kept opening while I carried her. What did she look like after three weeks, eh? What did she look like?'

He picked up the chair in front of him and swung with it as I lifted the siphon. They jarred in mid-air and the siphon slid down the wood, hit his fingers. The chair dropped but the siphon was knocked out of my hands. Across the falling stuff I jumped at him, glad now of this; we fell to the floor, rolled over. I knocked his fingers from my throat, got his; he tried to drag himself away, I hung on, glad of it, glad of it.

Something hit me across the eyes like blindness and fell beside me, the siphon; he thrust himself clear and was on top; at the third try he got his fingers where he wanted; they were slippery, sticky, but they held and tightened.

I plucked at his face and he stretched out of reach. Pressure on my neck stopped the blood. I knew, so far as knowledge was still there, that this last protest was over and with it the expiation; Lynn was waiting; body and soul I was hers; the skin had pulled away from the fingers and no air was left. The hangman's noose slackened as I died; like finding the reprieve of eternity.

Ray French was standing over me and the room focused occasionally and he'd swung away, was moving away, three, four steps while some sort of air passed like whooping-cough through my throat. I moved my head an inch and that brought sounds and pain back. Someone was putting a key in the door.

It came open as Ray faced it. His hand was dripping blood. A man I knew came in, a middle-aged man dressed like a shop-walker, with a face like a prison gaoler. And there was another man, and behind them someone from the hotel.

Ray said: 'Stay where you are.'

The man said sombrely: 'Look, Mr. French, I'd advise you to do nothing silly.' He glanced at me. 'Hobbs . . .'

The man behind him began to move but Ray said again: 'Stay where you are.'

No one stirred for a few seconds. Flash point had to come, but we suffered a temporary preservation from it, a photographic embalming of the moment before. Then Sergeant Baker took another step.

'I'll have to ask you to be reasonable, Mr. French. In the first place——'

Ray turned sharply and walked out of the french windows. Baker shouted and leapt after him but it was too late. There was a shadow on the balcony and then no shadow. He might have de-materialised, because there was no other sound, no cry, and we were too high even to hear the fall.

26

It was dark as I came out into Whitehall, and the rain had cleared at last. I didn't know the time because my watch had stopped at twenty-five to six; the glass was starred, a finger broken. It had become a stop-watch pointing the time of Ray's suicide.

It was dark and the rain had cleared, and my head still thumped between the eyes and I walked with a limp. Baker had offered me a car as far as Letherton but I'd said no, I'd stay in London to-night. 'I think it will be all right, Mr. Granville,' he'd said; 'but don't go far away until after the inquest, *please*. Perhaps I can call on you to-morrow?' A formidable person, Baker. The sandwiches I'd eaten in his office might have been lead-lined, and I couldn't feel yet that it was all right; everything had happened too quickly; and anyway the all right that Baker spoke of covered the narrowest field and left all the most complicated issues outside.

I turned up towards Trafalgar Square. They'd booked me a room by telephone at the usual hotel and had offered to run me there, but I said I'd walk. So I walked.

Baker had said: 'Your phone call to Mrs. Curtis just did the trick; we had the line tapped by then; I'd just got back to the Yard when the message came. Lucky for you. . . . It's a bad thing to conceal things from the police, Mr. Granville.'

Conceal things from the police. I'd just signed a statement in which nothing was concealed except all the things that counted—such as my hurt from Lynn and my love for Stella and my overriding obligation to . . . 'You've a good friend in Dr. Curtis. If it hadn't been for him. An inspired guess of his about French and Miss du Caine. Of course it was more than a guess. When I saw him this afternoon he gave me his reasons. No proof as we need it, but it has helped us to *find* the proof.'

I passed the R. U. S. Museum and crossed Horse Guards Avenue. Someone stared at the plaster on my forehead, and I stopped at the corner to look for a taxi, because I found walking wasn't in my line after all. But none came so I went on.

While I was having first-aid treatment Baker had been to see Margot du Caine.

'I had the greatest difficulty in persuading her to talk,' he said. 'Human nature's a strange thing. She was very distraught, appears now to be blaming herself and blaming her mother that she didn't marry him after all.' He paused for a while, brooding. 'You see, she loved him.'

I said: 'So did Lynn. . . .'

'Of course Miss du Caine had nothing to do with the murder, but she was in French's flat when he came back from visiting your wife late that Thursday afternoon. He'd had an appointment with her at five and hadn't turned up, so she'd gone round to his flat. He came back about six carrying the suit-case with your wife's initials on it, with scratches down his face, and coal dust on his shirt and

202

sleeves. It's not surprising, I suppose, that he didn't linger a second longer than he could help at your house after doing what he had done, or that he should want to wait until dusk before planting your wife's suit-case in her London flat. But Miss du Caine's unexpected presence put him on the spot. He told her he'd had a car accident with a coal lorry, he being with your wife in her car. The du Caine girl quarrelled with him because he'd promised not to see Mrs. Granville again, but she swallowed his story. No doubt French saw the possibilities and the danger right away. For him it became a race against time, whether he could marry Miss du Caine before the body was discovered. To that end he went to every length to keep your wife "alive".'

I crossed Whitehall and skirted Trafalgar Square. Three buses in line came round the corner, sweeping and speeding like fire-engines. A clock was striking; Big Ben; I stopped and counted. Eleven. Later than I thought.

I said to myself, I'm free, there's no longer any real danger at all. But it wasn't Baker or Margot du Caine I had to thank; it was John. It was his moves. . . .

I said to myself, I'm free; the shadow's gone; I'm free; I have to say it over and over again to try to believe it; because in my heart I know it's not true.

Or only superficially true. Because all the time this threat of arrest for Lynn's murder had been a sort of façade, behind which the real tensions had been mounting and maturing.

I thought, Lynn is gone but I still owe for Lynn. And if John is not yet gone he has made the unrepayable gesture. . . .

I limped up the Haymarket. The cinemas had all emptied and the streets were thinning. Just ahead were the electric fireworks of Piccadilly Circus tirelessly exploding their banal advice.

Their counsel to me would be simple and direct. Kruschen's for a top-heavy sense of obligation; Craven A for frayed nerves; Gordon's for loneliness. There was something to be said for over-simplification. Anyway, I knew the real cure for loneliness but I couldn't take it.

I got to the hotel and signed on and took the key. I went upstairs and lay on the bed and lit a cigarette and watched the smoke. I knew the cure for loneliness, and perhaps you found the answer to the other two complaints within the first. So it all depended really on what happened between me and Stella.

Over-simplification had a lot to recommend it here. I only had to wait. That was what it would boil down to in the end; I couldn't pretend anything else. Nothing finally could keep me away from her, not fire or storm or war, and if John now stood between us, and if his memory always would, yet I would take all that and any strings attached, to get the person I loved.

But I knew in my bones it wasn't going to be as easy as all that. The gap between her and me was greater than it had been a week ago and it would grow wider yet.

I lay back for a bit and my mind went over all the work I'd put into the last twelve months, seeing the new factory grow out of the grass, planning it, organising it, getting through the removal without complete chaos yet running into trouble almost at once; fending off Frank Dawson's bitter rivalry with Read; Piper and Burgin and all the complications and headaches of being half a scientist and half a business man and not quite either; the threatened strike. I thought of the survey equipment and the success of last night and what I'd lost in trying to win it. I thought of success generally, how much we sweated for it up every side-alley of life, how hard we tried for it and how little it eventually added up to. I thought of it all in a way I hadn't thought of it since that conversation with Simon, driving home from the night club with Lynn at my side before all this broke.

And, I thought, perhaps I've learned something since that night. Because I know now that life isn't a question of trying to get a quart *out* of a pint pot; it's more like finding the first drops to put into a pot of unknown size. Maybe that was an advance, thinking that. At least it seemed to lead somewhere, because I suddenly knew now what I'd got to do.

If I wanted to keep any of the things I cared about, I'd first got to learn to give them up. A primary law, that; and it operated in different ways at all stages of the game.

I'd got to grow up. I'd got to learn to break with the habit of grabbing at toys. Perhaps few enough people learned it, but for some reason I had to be one of them. Then perhaps later ... But later had to take care of itself. Take therefore no thought for the morrow.... Was that what it meant?

I picked up the phone and gave a Didcot number.

After about five minutes a voice said 'Thurston.'

I said: 'This is Granville. Sorry to phone you so late and at your private number but there was something I wanted to get settled. D'you think you could get hold of Bennett tonight?'

'What? Well ... It's a bit late, isn't it? I'll be seeing him first thing in the morning.'

'... Yes, all right. I want you to give him a message. Tell him I'll go to Africa with the survey stuff. Tell him I'm ready to start when he says.'

'You've decided to go?' Thurston sounded surprised.

'Yes.'

'What about your factory? Will it be able to carry on?'

'I think so.'

There was a pause. He said: 'By the way, did your manager get in touch with you?'

'Who? Read? No.'

'He phoned me this morning. Apparently he'd been trying to get in touch with you since yesterday morning and didn't know you were in Wales. Have you been threatened with some sort of a works stoppage?'

'A strike. Yes.'

'Well, he told me to tell you if I saw you. It's off.'

'Off ...'

'There was some sort of a vote, he said, and it went the right way.'

'Oh. ...'

Another pause. We were both thinking. He said: 'Does

that affect in any way your decision to go with the survey stuff?'

'No.'

'Look, Mike, let me make this quite plain. You've no need to do this to put yourself right with Harwell. You've done that. Bennett should have made that clear. Your going to the Sudan can't make you any better thought of than you are right now.'

'He did make it clear. That's not the reason I'm going. I want to. I want to see this thing through.'

'Yes, I know how you feel. I might feel the same in your shoes. But all the same I think you're making a mistake. Bennett should never have asked you.'

'Why not?'

'Because you're not a civil servant on a guaranteed salary—you're a scientific business man at a delicately balanced point in his business career. This strike scare only shows how much you need to be on hand. Of course it would be a great help to everyone concerned to have you out on the survey—no one's denying that for a moment—but you have other responsibilities, not only to the establishments but to yourself. No one has the right to demand that you give those up.'

I said: 'No one's demanding it, David—except myself.' He didn't reply. After a minute I went on: 'I can't explain it to you more than by saying that this is the thing I have to do.'

We talked for a minute or two and then I put the receiver down.

I put my cigarette down. I eased the plaster on my forehead and lay staring at the ceiling. I don't often remember feeling more alone. There was a fly on the ceiling walking upside down dogged by a tiny shadow cast by the light. It seemed just then that he probably knew quite as much as I did about the equilibrium of the world.

I picked up the receiver again to telephone my love.